Meet the officers of the Rocky Mountain K-9 Unit series and their brave K-9 partners

Officer: Gavin Walker

K-9 Partner: Koda the Malinois

Assignment: Keep veterinarian Dr. Sydney Jones safe

Officer: Victor Abrams

K-9 Partner: Cleo the Labrador

Assignment: Help K-9 admin Jodie Chen figure out who killed a woman who came to her for help

With over seventy books published and millions in print, **Lenora Worth** writes award-winning romance and romantic suspense. Three of her books were finalists for the ACFW Carol Awards, and her Love Inspired Suspense novel *Body of Evidence* became a *New York Times* bestseller. Her novella in *Mistletoe Kisses* made her a *USA TODAY* bestselling author. Lenora goes on adventures with her retired husband, Don, and enjoys reading, baking and shopping...especially shoe shopping.

Katy Lee writes suspenseful romances that thrill and inspire. She believes every story should stir and satisfy the reader—from the edge of their seat. A native New Englander, Katy loves to knit warm woolly things. She enjoys traveling the side roads and exploring the locals' hideaways. A homeschooling mom of three competitive swimmers, Katy often writes from the stands while cheering them on. Visit Katy at katyleebooks.com.

CHRISTMAS K-9 UNIT HEROES

LENORA WORTH
KATY LEE

LOVE INSPIRED SUSPENSE
INSPIRATIONAL ROMANCE

Special thanks and acknowledgment are given to Lenora Worth and Katy Lee for their contributions to the Rocky Mountain K-9 Unit miniseries.

LOVE INSPIRED® SUSPENSE
INSPIRATIONAL ROMANCE

ISBN-13: 978-1-335-58738-1

Christmas K-9 Unit Heroes

Copyright © 2022 by Harlequin Enterprises ULC

Hidden Christmas Danger
Copyright © 2022 by Harlequin Enterprises ULC

Silent Night Explosion
Copyright © 2022 by Harlequin Enterprises ULC

For questions and comments about the quality of this book, please contact us at CustomerService@Harlequin.com.

Love Inspired
22 Adelaide St. West, 41st Floor
Toronto, Ontario M5H 4E3, Canada
www.LoveInspired.com

Printed in U.S.A.

CONTENTS

HIDDEN CHRISTMAS DANGER

Lenora Worth

To Emily Rodmell, a great editor.
Thank you for always pushing me to write my best stories.
I am grateful for your hard work!

Thy right hand, O Lord, is become glorious in power:
thy right hand, O Lord, hath dashed in pieces the enemy.
—*Exodus* 15:6

ONE

The two dogs in the kennel went wild.

Dr. Sydney Jones glanced up from the paperwork she'd been trying to finish. She checked the clock on the wall over her desk at the Rocky Mountain K-9 Unit Headquarters in Denver, where she worked on a part-time basis as the official veterinarian with the K-9 officer dogs.

Ten at night.

Wow, where had the time gone? Again, she recognized Shiloh's bark, followed by Cleo's less aggressive one. Shiloh could sense something off, she supposed. The black Lab hadn't made the K-9 team due to a lack of ability to stay focused, but he'd been good at learning sign language.

Sydney decided she'd go and calm both dogs. She was used to working late here several times a week after she left her clinic and had plans to take some downtime for the upcoming holidays. She'd scheduled people to watch the one dog they were boarding here through Christmas, and she'd already lined up help for the Jones Veterinary Clinic, which she owned and wasn't far from here. She'd stay close, do some hiking, enjoy Christmas with friends she'd met at the dog park. A nice, quiet holiday. Her chaotic family back in Kansas wouldn't even miss her. Her sisters and brothers had their own lives now, same as her.

She got up and walked past the tiny Christmas tree

holding pet-inspired ornaments and dog-shaped twinkling lights to head down the hallway to the kennels. Halfway there, she heard a shattering noise and more fierce barking. She had unexpected company.

Hurrying toward the dogs, her only intent was to stop any intruders. She'd open the kennels and then she'd call for help. Shiloh might hesitate in responding, but Cleo had years of service under her belt in the US Navy and would know what to do. Their barks could scare someone if she let them out. Just in case, she grabbed the nearest thing she could use as a weapon—a syringe lying by a vial of ketamine. Sydney quickly drew some of the liquid into the syringe and dropped it into the deep pocket of her lab coat.

Force of habit, because she'd worked in a large animal clinic high up in the mountains before moving to Denver to open her own practice, and later becoming the official vet for the RMKU. She knew a small dose could take effect quickly and knock out a feral animal or a dangerous human.

She'd reached the door to the exam rooms and the inside kennels near the training yard when she heard the click of a gun. A sweaty hand grabbed her around the neck. Realizing someone had come through the unlocked back door, she inhaled a gasp.

"Do not move."

She nodded, her pulse racing while her mind worked to comprehend how she could get out of this situation. She didn't dare go for the tranquilizer now.

She had no way to alert anyone.

With the holidays approaching, the team only had a skeleton crew working this weekend. She was on her own unless someone from the RMKU building heard the dogs barking.

That would teach her not to work so late again.

"What do you want?" she asked, thinking if she could get him talking, she'd be able to distract him.

"I need a doctor. You available?" He pushed the gun tighter against her ribs.

"Yes."

"Good answer."

"But you might have noticed, I treat animals, not humans."

Sometimes humans, however, did act like animals. Worse than animals.

Shoving her forward while he still held her, he said, "Get me to an exam room. I've been stabbed."

"Okay." She pointed ahead. "Next to the kennel room."

He heaved a hot breath that seared her skin. "Can you make those dogs shut up?"

"No. They have a high sense of smell, and they've picked up your scent." Or one of his many scents, none too pleasant. They'd also picked up on his anxiety, his panic, his desperation.

"I know how to handle that." He pointed the gun toward the kennel room.

"No," she said. "You will not hurt those animals. I'll do whatever you need, but please don't do anything to the K-9s."

He grunted while she studied the hand on her arm. A tattoo or stamp of some kind covered his left forearm. A circle with swirls merging together, topped with the letters MSA. She had yet to see his face.

"Okay, then," he said, his voice husky with pain. "You do as I say, and I'll leave the puppy dogs alone. Deal?"

"Deal." She'd get him on a table in the one exam room that could be seen from the hallway door, and check his wound, then find a way to shoot him up with the tranquilizer hidden in her pocket. Because she had a feeling that once she'd stitched him up, he might kill her, anyway. She'd seen his tattoo.

* * *

K-9 Officer Gavin Walker and his all-purpose Malinois, Koda, made the rounds of the RMKU headquarters perimeter, mainly to get some fresh air and exercise. Located next to the training facility on the outskirts of Denver, the RMKU building wasn't fancy, but it held a fluid mobile unit. The team assisted the FBI with difficult cases across the Rocky Mountain region—Wyoming, Montana, Idaho, Colorado and New Mexico. Gavin had transferred here a few months ago from the New Mexico state police K-9 unit, thanks to his buddy, and the Rocky Mountain unit's leader, Sergeant Tyson Wilkes.

Gavin liked the quiet of being the lone officer on duty tonight. With snow covering the outer fringes of the parking lot and outbuildings, he felt cocooned and at peace. Rare for him to feel that way. He'd come to the team late, and while he'd had lots of experience in New Mexico and he'd also served as an army ranger with Tyson, he was still one of the new members on the team, a probie. That meant he got holiday duty. But he'd readily agreed. Gavin had no family here and his parents were on a trip to Europe they'd been planning for years. He'd sent them a nice check to help cover the expenses.

"I'll see you when you get home in January, and we can celebrate Christmas then," he'd told his mom. "Go and have fun. I'll hang with my friends here."

He'd had plenty of invitations for Christmas dinner, so he didn't feel so bad. And he'd planned a couple of hiking trips, something he'd come to love about living in the Rockies. The seasoned team members all needed a break, anyway, after dealing with several tough ongoing cases for most of this year.

"Right, Koda? We'll be fine."

His constant companion let out a soft woof of approval. They walked the perimeter of the big open parking lot, then moved toward the parking garage off to the side. Pretty much empty now. But Gavin spotted one car still there.

Doc Sydney Jones. The veterinarian seemed to always work late. She loved the K-9s and treated each one with respect and tough love. Tough described her, too. With short brown hair that lifted in waves against her chin and forehead, she had a gamine look, but her deep brown eyes gave away nothing. She seemed to like animals more than humans. Quiet, to the point and intriguing, she had her own practice, but she spent a lot of time here, too, working with the K-9s. He and Koda managed to visit her every now and then, even when neither of them needed a checkup. Gavin liked being around her because she didn't push any buttons and she didn't trigger any issues.

She was just Doc Sydney. Easy to talk to, tough to argue with and always concerned for the team's four-legged partners.

After spotting her blue SUV, Gavin glanced toward the animal hospital and saw a light burning.

"Koda, want to go see Doc?"

The big Malinois yelped and lifted his head, his nose in the air, his ears up. Then he growled low.

Gavin froze. What scent had Koda picked up?

"What is it, boy?"

Koda stood still, trembling, his eyes on the medical building. Gavin listened. When he heard dogs barking, he tugged at Koda. "Let's go check."

Sydney told herself to remain calm. But when the man holding her whirled her around, she had to hide her fear. He was wearing a black buff-type stretchy cloth over his face. The material hung down around his neck and he had on a dark beanie that didn't show much of his head. She noted a beat-up canvas barn jacket and dirty jeans over heavy work boots.

"Listen, lady," he said, favoring his left side, "don't even think about knocking me out with some drug or hitting me over the head. You need to stitch me up so I can get out of here."

Sydney nodded in agreement, her mind staying two steps ahead while she considered her options. "I'll treat you, but if you want stitches, I'll have to give you a local anesthetic at least."

"No."

"Trust me, it will hurt. I'll have to use needle holders and forceps and I'll be suturing a six-inch gash, not to mention the wound could cause internal bleeding in a major organ."

She couldn't tell for sure, but he probably wouldn't be walking if the knife had hit his spleen or kidneys. He'd be lying somewhere bleeding out. She didn't share that guess with him, however. She wanted him scared enough to let her use something local for the pain.

His eyes bulged but he showed her the gun again. "Something mild," he said. "I have to keep moving."

"Is someone after you?"

He put a finger to his lips.

She mouthed, "Do you need help?"

He shook his head. "Hurry, lady."

Then he mouthed, "Sorry."

He grunted and got up on the table, the gun still on her. "No questions. Get my jacket open and get to work."

Sydney did as he said. When she saw the wound, her gaze shot up to him. "One more inch and you'd be dead. The knife just missed your kidneys."

"Yeah, I know." He shrugged. "I need you to do this, and quick, before someone finds me."

"Will they finish the job?" she whispered.

He looked up at her and gave her a wry, pain-filled smile. "They'll finish what I came here to do."

"And what is that?"

"I said no more questions." Then he thought better. He pulled her close and whispered in her ear. "I guess you might need to know, in case I die, or *you* try to kill me."

"Know what?" she asked, apprehension dancing against her nerves.

"They sent me to kill you, but I got into some trouble before I could do the job. I blinked and they didn't like that. They made sure I'd *have* to come here."

Sydney took in a breath, hot dread flowing through her burning nerves. Someone wanted her dead? "And if I save you, will you still kill me?"

He laughed and held the gun high. "What do you think? The only reason you're alive now is because I'm not ready to die. Now stitch me up and we'll see which one of us makes it through the night."

TWO

Gavin and Koda slipped through the night without making any noise. They both knew the drill. Gavin had his gun out and ready as he moved behind the small building where Doc Jones took care of the dogs. Located near the training yard and positioned near a high chain-link fence that kept the dogs in and strangers out, it held a long row of open-wire kennels. But only two dogs were here tonight, and they were barking aggressively *inside* the vet building.

"Let's see what we find," Gavin whispered. Then he gave Koda the silent command, holding his arm out and down so the dog would understand.

Koda still trembled but stayed quiet.

"Good boy," Gavin whispered as he shadowed the building until he could find a window. When he didn't see Sydney at her corner desk, he moved on to the kennel room. The windows were high here, so he had to stretch to get a glance inside.

The K-9s being boarded were fidgeting back and forth, their barks indicating their increased agitation. They must have picked up a foreign scent, same as Koda.

Gavin moved around the corner of the building to the back door, where a small glass pane allowed him to see straight into one of the exam rooms. Immediately, he found footprints in the mud and snow. Large cratered shoe prints.

He'd get back to that later. Working around them so he didn't disturb the prints, he tried to see inside the window.

When he spotted Sydney standing over a man who was wearing a dark face mask and holding a gun, Gavin moved back before the stranger saw him. Taking another quick glance, he summed up the situation. The man's bloody shirt was open and revealed a deep wound covering the left stomach area. Sydney moved quickly back and forth, bringing a small metal bowl and what looked like surgical supplies to a rolling tray next to the exam bed.

She was preparing to stitch up his wound.

Gavin put his hand on the doorknob. Locked.

He watched again as Sydney, cool and efficient, went about her business. But she had to be terrified inside. And he had to do something, anything, to help her.

He went around the building, trying keypads, but he didn't know the code to the tiny hospital's front door. No way in through the back door. How had the intruder gained entry?

Finally, Gavin tried a window in the storage room, and after he tugged and grunted, he managed to get it up enough that he and Koda could slip inside.

The dogs increased their barking, but Gavin couldn't control that now. He and Koda crept to the door of the room and Gavin silently turned the knob. It wasn't locked. No drugs in here, just boxes of latex gloves, papers for the exam tables and towels. He creaked the door open an inch.

"You need to see a surgeon." It was Sydney, talking to the intruder. "This is deep, and you could be bleeding internally."

"Then stitch me up," the man said, his voice weak now. "I have to get away from here."

"I'm about to inject a local anesthetic," she said. "It will numb the area. That's the best I can do."

"Then do it. I need to stay awake."

Sydney kept him talking while she carefully injected something around the wound. "So you can shoot me, you mean?"

Gavin hissed a breath. The man wanted to kill the doc? *Nope, not gonna happen.*

"I have to kill you," the man explained, wincing as the needle did its job. "They'll want proof I did it."

"And once they get that proof, you'll be eliminated, too?"

"I told you no more questions."

The man shook his head and waved the gun in the air. Then he whispered, "Please."

Gavin was amazed that Sydney was able to ignore the gun and keep right on cleaning the wound. He formed a plan—he'd have Koda head down the hallway and then he'd call for the big dog to guard.

That would startle the gunman and the doctor, but it might give him enough time to distract the guy and give Sydney time to duck or jam another needle into the intruder somehow.

Gavin waited a couple of minutes then glanced at Koda. "Ready, boy?"

The dog stood straight and ready.

"Okay then, let's get the doc out of here."

He opened the door and whispered, "Go." Waited two more beats and then shouted as loud as he could, "Guard!"

The other dogs echoed barks of approval while Koda jumped into the air at a fast trot and stopped just at the entrance to the exam room. The doctor and the man both turned around, surprise registering on their faces.

Sydney spotted Gavin coming up the hallway, her eyes going wide with relief.

The man on the table tried to reach out and grab her, but she jumped back. "That's enough. You shoot me now, and my friend Koda will bite you and he won't let go. Then his partner will make sure you do die on this table."

Then she gave Gavin a warning stare. "Wait."

Gavin didn't dare acknowledge her signal.

The patient groaned and tried to stand, but shock and the element of surprise, coupled with whatever she'd given him, had him dizzy and still in pain. He lifted his gun and aimed it straight at Dr. Jones as Gavin came barreling through the door.

"Stop. Drop the gun. Or my partner will make mincemeat of your arm."

The man cursed and groaned. "I can't do that. They'll kill me."

Gavin advanced a little farther. "I'll shoot you on the spot if you don't do as I say."

The man raised the gun. Koda growled low. Gavin checked Sydney, but she stood still, waiting. Before either of them could shoot, the man whispered, "Bridges," and passed out cold, sending the supply tray flying while he hit the floor with a thud, his gun slipping out of his hand.

"Guard," Gavin called to Koda. Then he hurried to Sydney. "Hey, Doc, it's over. You're safe now."

Sydney nodded. Then she sank back against the counter. "Thank you. I wasn't sure when the tranquilizer would kick in."

Impressed, Gavin gave her a lift of his chin, then checked the man's pulse. "Weak. I'm calling for an ambulance."

Then he turned to her and looked her over. "Really, Doc, you weren't sure about the anesthetic?"

"It seemed like a good idea at the time, and it did work. His injury wasn't as bad as I let on, but I had to convince him somehow so I could inject a dose of ketamine."

Gavin smiled. The woman had guts, he'd give her that. "Let's get you a place to sit. I'll take care of your intruder."

She lifted her head, the dark silky bangs curling over

her eyes hiding her fear. "He came here to kill me, Gavin," she said. "But he needed medical help first."

"I heard," Gavin replied. "I also heard him say 'Bridges' before he went down. Any idea what that means?"

She shook her head. "Michael Bridges is the FBI special agent in charge. Him, maybe?"

"That's what I'm thinking, too," Gavin said. "We both know Michael Bridges is the best. He wouldn't send anyone to kill you."

"This man was scared," she said. "He kept whispering, as if afraid someone was listening."

Gavin leaned over the man and checked him. "No wires or bugs that I can find." Then he looked up at her. "I'll call SAC Bridges right away."

"Yes, do your job." She stood, wobbled a bit.

Gavin caught her, his voice husky in her ear. "Listen, you're safe, you're okay now, all right?"

She blinked, took a deep breath and then looked up at Gavin. "Who would want to kill me?"

Gavin couldn't answer that question yet, but he'd find the answers she needed.

He held her steady and replied, "I don't know, but we're gonna find out, I can promise you that." Then he added, "And meantime, I don't plan on leaving your side."

THREE

Sydney sat in a hospital waiting room with a police officer standing across from her. Nothing like having your life threatened a few weeks before Christmas. She'd tried to pray for calm and here she sat, one leg crossed over the other swinging in a nervous wave of fear. She wasn't accustomed to fear. But each time she thought of that man holding a gun on her, his hands shoving her, his gravelly voice ordering her around, she got scared all over again. Scared and mad. Angry. She felt more consumed by anger than fear. Who would want to target a veterinarian? What purpose would killing her have?

She thought over all the clients she'd helped through the years—with horses, dogs, cats, birds, turtles, even gerbils and pet mice. No one had ever come after her before. Most of her clients were happy with her work.

So she feared the worst—someone wanted her dead for some irrational reason.

Gavin Walker, on the other hand, seemed to have no fear.

Their earlier conversation, after the intruder had been taken away and the kennels had settled down, had gone something like this:

"You don't have to stick with me, Gavin. I'm used to

taking care of myself. I have a loaded gun in a safe box in my bedroom. I know how to use it."

"I'm sure you do, but someone wants you dead," Gavin answered with a no-nonsense stare. "I'm witness to that. I'm going to get permission to cover you twenty-four-seven."

"You'll need to sleep."

"I'm not good at sleeping."

"I like Koda, so there is that."

"Koda likes you," he said with a slight smile. "So there is that." He stood. "I'm going to try and talk to your would-be killer one more time." Then he told Koda to stay.

Now, the black-and-tan Malinois was sitting here staring up at her, as his human partner had commanded. She let the dog do his job, but she wanted to grab Koda and hug him tight. But that would go against protocol. And it would only confuse the dog and make the officer guarding her frown.

And Gavin—he was another matter. Good-looking in that cool, tormented way that shouted "bad boy," his eyes were a startling shade of blue, his hair a messy, silky black and he was a good officer and who worked great with Koda. So she couldn't label him as a bad boy. She wasn't sure how to label him, really. Sydney and Gavin had talked a lot about the officer dogs, the work they both did, the sun and the stars, football, mountains and just about anything that had nothing to do with personal stuff. But if he stayed on her like glue, they'd have to get to know each other. That made her nervous.

He came out of the room where they were holding her attacker, his frown showing he wasn't happy.

"What did he say?" she asked, standing to stretch. Koda stood and got between her and the long hospital corridor. "Did he explain why he mentioned Bridges?"

Gavin motioned her to sit and told Koda to do the same.

"His name is Rick Samuels, but that could be an alias," Gavin said, his voice quiet but deep. "Does that name mean anything to you?"

She shook her head. "I don't know the name."

Gavin glanced around. "There's more, Doc."

"Tell me."

"He says he's an informant for the FBI. That's the first shocker. The second—he immediately asked again to speak to SAC Michael Bridges. He also told me he's gotten in too deep with an off-the-radar organization—MSA. Heard of it?"

Sydney let out a gasp. "The Mountain Scouts Association?"

"Yep. So you do know about this group?"

"I used to," she said, the dread in her head rushing a warning beat through her heart. "The group started decades ago as a legitimate outdoor club that served as scouts for hunters, fishermen, mountain hikes and climbing, shooting the rapids—anything to do with the outdoors throughout the western states. But over the last decade or so, it's turned into something more sinister." She took a breath. "I hear they deal in buying and selling illegal drugs and weapons."

Gavin grunted. "That's what Samuels told me, too. I've put in a call to SAC Bridges. He'll verify if Samuels is telling the truth about being an informant. Sometimes, even the best informants go bad. But if what he's telling me is the truth, Samuels has a target on his back now."

SAC Bridges would want to get to the bottom of this.

"But why did they send him to kill me?" Sydney asked, her mind whirling with possibilities that she didn't want to voice.

"That, we don't know. Samuels was supposed to kill you, but he balked at the assignment. They stabbed him right outside our compound and sent him to you—a ruse to get him inside. And they did tell him if he didn't do the job, they'd kill him. I think we scared them off since we found no one waiting around anywhere near the compound."

"I believe that part," Sydney said. "He told me they'd kill him if he failed, and they'd kill me if I live. But *they* conveniently got away."

Gavin did another visual swept of the long, empty hallway. "And that's why I asked SAC Bridges if I could guard you while I work on this case."

Sydney didn't argue. "I appreciate that, Gavin. I have to admit this is concerning."

"Concerning? Doc, someone wants to kill you. You have a right to be concerned and scared and angry and confused."

"You covered it all," she replied, grateful he'd been nearby and had heard the kenneled dogs barking. Deciding she wouldn't look a gift horse in the mouth, she gave him an appreciative smile. "Gavin, I wouldn't be here if you hadn't come along."

"Oh, I don't know about that. You have a way with tranquilizer needles," he teased.

He offered her a hand and she stood up again. "How 'bout we find something to eat? I'm starving. And a good meal might make us both more relaxed and reasonable."

Was she being unreasonable? Wouldn't be the first time someone had thought that about her.

Sydney hadn't thought about food but now that she knew Rick Samuels couldn't hurt her, she did feel hungry. "Where will we go? What if they're watching?"

Gavin leaned close. "My place," he said. "I have a roundabout way of getting there. I'll make sure we take the long way back."

Then he went to the guard and issued some orders.

Sydney followed him to the elevator and down to the parking garage. Gavin put Koda on alert, and the Malinois sniffed the cold cement floor as well as the chilly air. They made it to Gavin's official SUV. He opened the hatch with a remote key and Koda hopped in and did a circle, then lay down.

"He's such a good K-9," she said once they were safely inside. "I know all-purpose dogs can be dangerous because they're taught to bite on command, but Koda is such a sweetheart."

"Do you say that about all your K-9 patients?" Gavin asked.

"Probably, but Koda is one of my buddies. He was a bit fidgety when you first brought him here. Now, he's settled. And I think you're beginning to feel the same."

"And I wasn't taught to bite," he said with a crooked smile.

"We're all glad about that."

Gavin glanced over at her. "I suppose I do feel settled, at that. But you're the first case I've taken on here by myself. I don't want to mess this up, Doc."

"Call me Sydney," she said. Then she added, "I trust you, Gavin. And now I'm depending on you to keep me safe. But I should warn you, I'm also planning to keep myself safe."

Gavin pulled out into traffic, then glanced over at her. "Yeah, and that scares me almost as much as trying to find these people who're after you, Sydney."

FOUR

Gavin had circled around his apartment complex before finally deciding they were safe. At least his place wasn't as isolated as hers. While they'd waited at the hospital, he'd mapped out her cabin location and noted the trail of a road and the rocky terrain all around. Easy for someone to sneak up on her.

He'd chosen a home near a dog park so he could exercise Koda, but he liked to go late at night or early in the morning. He had a one-bedroom apartment in a complex where all the town houses looked about the same. He had a small, enclosed backyard for Koda, too, and a nice mountain view when he had time to actually sit and look at it.

"You live close to the city," Sydney said as he pulled up in front of the one-car garage that he'd turned into a workout room. "I can see why you brought me here instead of taking me to my place."

"You can go back there once it's cleared," he said. "You'll need to get a security system."

She held a hand to the dashboard. "I never dreamed of having one, of needing much security."

"Koda and I will be there with you until this is over, so I can help you install one."

The Malinois let out a soft woof.

"I don't want to live in fear," she said, her words quiet

but full of resolve. "I hope this is over soon." Then she shrugged. "I was looking forward to a few quiet days during Christmas."

"I'll do my best to make sure you get them," he said. "Stay there until I get Koda out."

She sat and waited, but Gavin and Koda didn't waste any time getting to her.

"Koda is serious about his duties," she said, watching as the dog lifted his nose and did a full sniff for any threats.

"We both are," Gavin told her once he felt sure Koda hadn't picked up any unusual scents.

"Thank you," she said after they'd cleared the area. "I'll be forever grateful to you two."

"Not exactly the best way to bring us together," he said, then instantly regretted it when her eyes went wide. "I mean, if we were social after work, this would not be my first choice on making that happen. Not that we would ever socialize after work."

She actually smiled. "Dug yourself into that hole good and deep, Officer Walker."

"Uh, call me Gavin and…yeah, I pretty much blew that comforting thought."

"It is comforting," she said as he guided her toward the apartment door and did a scan of the surrounding town houses—there were four homes to each unit of the vast complex. "And we don't have to socialize. I can stay in another part of the apartment."

"Sorry on that, Doc. I have one bedroom and after I wash some linens and clean it up, you'll have to take that."

"And where will you stay?" she asked at the door.

"On the couch. It's actually almost as comfortable as the bed."

"I can't do that," she said, her eyes as dark as the night. "I mean, I can't let you take the couch."

"I keep watch better from the couch. Koda will sleep in his bed near you."

She didn't look so sure as they entered his place. "I hate this."

"I know it's not the best solution, and this is certainly not a fancy chateau, but I can protect you until we hear more."

"It's not your home I'm protesting, Gavin," she said, glancing around at unpacked boxes and a sparse arrangement of old furniture. "It's this—hiding out, worried about being killed, not understanding who is after me."

Gavin shut the door, locked it, sent Koda ahead to inspect the bedroom and bath down the hallway, then turned to her. "I'll clear your home tomorrow. I have officers watching it tonight, okay. You can't be there if someone shows up, but our people will handle it. Hopefully, I'll get you home soon."

"I don't mean to sound ungrateful after I just told you how grateful I am," she replied, her gaze settling on the kitchen. "Do you mind if I cook?"

Gavin did an about-face. "You want to cook, here, now?"

"Yes. Cooking helps me calm down. That is, if you have anything cookable."

"Let me see." He moved past her into the small galley kitchen and opened the tiny refrigerator. "I have skirt steak I'd planned to grill this weekend and some frozen vegetables my mom always insists I get."

"I can work with that," she said, her smile more relaxed.

He looked in the one cabinet he called a pantry. "Hey, I have tortilla chips and a jar of salsa, too."

"We can have a mash-up of grilled steak and vegetables with chips. I only need a big pan to sauté everything."

He provided a pan. "You're amazing."

"No, I'm nervous and out of my element, and kinda hungry," she said. "You go freshen up."

"Yes, ma'am. But Koda stays with you."

Koda returned and glanced from one to the other.

"Stay. Guard," Gavin said.

The dog sat back on his haunches and stared at Sydney.

"He likes watching out for you," Gavin said.

"I like that he's watching out for me," she replied.

"I'll be back soon."

"We'll stay here, right, Koda."

Koda woofed low and didn't move an inch.

"Such a good boy," Sydney said, her voice husky, her worries gone now.

It was easy to pretend they were only having dinner together. Not so easy to forget seeing her with that dangerous man tonight. Rick Samuels might be an informant for the FBI, but something had gone wrong with that scenario.

Gavin hurried to take a shower, but on the way, he had a flash of a daydream. Her, him and Koda on a mountainside. Happy.

Silly, of course. He had to save the woman's life, not spend time daydreaming about her. But…that had been a nice thought. One he'd save for a later time.

She seasoned the slender skirt steak, then threw in the green and red peppers and onions she'd thawed and drained and patted dry. She'd found some butter in the refrigerator, so she threw in a hunk of that, too. The kitchen smelled wonderful, and her anxiety cooled to a low-to-medium status. Trying not to think about what she'd been through, she glanced at the clock.

Close to midnight. No wonder she was so hungry and antsy. She pulled out the bag of chips and found the salsa. Why did men love chips and salsa so much?

She'd noticed he didn't have any decorations up or even

a Christmas tree. Sydney loved Christmas. Maybe she could help Gavin find his holiday spirit. But only after the people after her were caught and sent to jail. She spotted a picture of Gavin with his mother and father. She'd heard his mother was Hispanic. Gavin had her dark hair, but he had his father's blue eyes.

When a clean, woodsy scent came from the hallway, she turned to find Gavin in an old T-shirt and jeans, his hair still damp, and the sight took her mind from anxiety to attraction.

She'd considered him a friend before, an officer who she ran into here and there at work. But now, she had to consider him as an attractive man. She'd never noticed him in this way. A way that made her heart do strange little leaps. How could that be possible after the night she'd had?

Nerves. That had to be it. Heightened danger brought out the dizzy nerves and the strange brain thoughts. Add to that, he'd saved her and helped her get away from that awful man.

They'd bonded, a natural result of being in danger together.

"Are you doing okay over there cooking?" he asked, after telling Koda to rest. Off duty now, Koda started dancing around.

"I'm calmer now, yes," she said, but her heart was thudding with a new awareness of this man.

Gavin was still on duty, but she sure appreciated him being out of uniform and more laid-back. Now if she could shut down these jitters and focus on the food, they might be able to figure out the reason she'd wound up here with him tonight.

Someone had planned to kill her.

FIVE

"A good meal," he said an hour later. They sat on the couch to be away from the windows. "You whipped that together so easily. I would have grilled it to a crisp and eaten it with just the salsa and chips."

"That's why your mom insists you buy frozen vegetables," she replied, glad for this reprieve from her fears and doubts. But she jumped each time she heard a noise or a car backfiring.

"Probably," he replied. "So before we dig in to the who and why of this case, what about your family?"

"What about them?"

"You said once in passing that you had a large family in Kansas."

"Yes, my parents and siblings still live there, but I moved away as soon as I could."

"So you left the fold?"

"The fold left me," she said. "A lot of infighting caused me to want out. That's why I like my privacy even now. I never had any privacy, caught in that middle between opposing forces."

Gavin gave her a long stare, his smile more of a lip twitch. "I have one brother and, yes, we fought but we're still close. I'm sorry you had a difficult childhood."

"I survived and I'm tough because of it."

"I can see that."

"What about you?" she asked. "You served your country."

"Just doing my job."

"Right." She sighed and grabbed her glass of water. "I always wanted to be a veterinarian. I grew up on a farm, so I've been around animals all my life. After I graduated, I got several offers to work for other vets, but I wanted my own office. So I looked at the map, studied the places I'd always wanted to go and wound up here. It wasn't easy. I did have to work for other people until I could take out a loan to buy my own clinic."

"About the other veterinarians you worked for—any reason one of them might be targeting you?"

"I got along great with the two I worked for. One in Greeley, who didn't want to retire, so I had to cover for him a lot. He died a month after he'd closed the clinic. So I found work here in Denver in a practice I loved, but the owner decided to move to Wyoming. He put the practice up for sale, but I couldn't afford to buy it. I found a building I could afford and started my own clinic. The bank gets most of my paycheck, so that's why I applied to help out here. Anyway, I can't think of anybody I'm associated with workwise or any of my clients, who would have a reason to want me dead."

"I can't imagine anyone wanting you dead, either," he said, his eyes holding hers. "Now we need to get personal about your life. Old friends, old boyfriends, anyone who ever had a dispute with you?"

Sydney shook her head. "I… I didn't date much in medical school and then work took over." She stopped, the one thought that had gone through her mind earlier nagging at her like a radar flashing in her head. "There is one ex-boyfriend."

* * *

Gavin sat up straight on the couch, causing Koda's ears to perk up. Frowning at Sydney, he said, "Okay, you might have led with that one."

"I—I didn't want to think about him, or the possibility that he could be behind this. His name is Mack Creston. We had a bad breakup when I decided to go out on my own. He was demanding and too overprotective and controlling. I balked at that since I'd left those such issues back home."

Gavin's phone pinged. He lifted a finger. "Hold that thought. I have to take this."

He watched as she nodded and reached out to Koda, letting him sniff her knuckles. The dog nudged her hand and waited for her to rub his head.

"Sir," Gavin said, knowing this couldn't be good. Bridges only called late at night if something had developed with a case.

"Gavin, I have bad news. Rick Samuels is dead."

"Dead?" Gavin glanced at Sydney. She stood and stared at him. "What happened?" Gavin asked.

"Someone got to him in the hospital," SAC Bridges replied. "The perpetrator ran out through the cafeteria kitchen door before anyone could catch him."

Gavin let out a tired sigh. "Okay, sir. Guess we start from scratch, unless you got anything else out of him."

"Nope. Look, the man was a good FB informant. He did the right thing and tried to get out of doing murder, but these people meant what they said to him." Bridges went quiet for a moment. "We've had our eyes on MSA for a while now and Samuels was a good inside man. I knew we had agents in there, but I don't have all the details. Also, he's been backstopped. We set up a whole new identity for him so I need to go over his records and reports. I've got people digging into the situation to see what's happening there."

Gavin heaved a sigh. "He had all the information, and he did drop hints, even with Sydney. But somebody didn't want him to tell the whole story. From what we've gathered, this club has gone from good to bad. Illegal gun and drug trafficking can't stay hidden for long."

"Nope." Bridges went quiet.

Gavin took that as a sign to finish up. "I remember his last words to us. He said they'd kill him, and now they have."

"He also said they'd kill Sydney, too, but he wouldn't give us anything more." Bridges grunted. "I've got to take this other call, Gavin."

"I haven't forgotten that threat. Keep us posted."

"I will. Oh, and Gavin, so far no one's messed with Sydney's house. But that could change soon, however. Be alert. They might come for both of you."

"Thank you, sir. We'll be careful."

Bridges had always been all business, but the last few times Gavin had talked to him, he'd been off somehow.

Gavin ended the call and went to Sydney, thinking he didn't have time to decipher the SAC's state of mind. "You heard?"

She nodded. "They were watching and waiting." Then she rubbed her arms. "And if they sent someone to the hospital to kill Samuels, they probably know I'm here with you."

He started checking windows and looking for cars he didn't recognize. "Stay down on the couch, Sydney. Just in case."

Koda stood when Gavin gave him a hand signal. The two of them checked every corner of the apartment. "I'm gonna call someone to scout the area, look for anybody who's out this late."

Sydney nodded, but he could see the dejection and concern in her eyes. How could he help her?

Gavin said a prayer as he scanned the backyard and the fence. Nothing. Nobody. He said another prayer as he went back to the front, refusing to give up.

"Gavin?"

He turned to Sydney. "It's okay. So far, nothing."

Then he heard a noise outside, the clattering of trash cans hitting against each other, a thump and more clashing of metal against metal.

SIX

Sydney's heart rate accelerated into high speed. What a nightmare. Had Mack finally found her? Not that she'd been hiding, but she'd tried to be low-key. And she'd believed he'd moved on, same as she had. He had hinted at Wyoming or maybe Canada, and that was the last she'd heard from him. She prayed this wasn't about him, that whoever wanted to kill her had nothing to do with her ex.

But instincts told her otherwise. He'd been a perfect fit with this kind of outdoors club. She should have seen all the signs that things were changing within the organization, but she'd been busy with work, and in her heart she'd thought maybe he did good things even if he treated her so badly. Always the first mistake.

Gavin put a finger to his lips and motioned her toward the bedroom. "Get in the closet and close the door."

She nodded and watched as he commanded Koda to guard her.

"Take Koda with you if you're going out there," she whispered.

"He stays with you. Shut the door."

Gavin slipped out the front door, probably to circle around the back. She glanced at Koda and knew he wouldn't let her leave this room. So she slid into the small closet and sank down with her head on her knees, but she kept the door cracked. "Thank you, Koda," she whispered. Then she said a prayer for Gavin to stay safe.

The fresh scent of Gavin's clothes surrounded her like a protective forest of evergreens. She took deep breaths and reached her hand out to search for some kind of weapon. Nothing but boots and sweaters on a shelf squeezed to the side. She could push the shelf toward an attacker.

When she heard footsteps hurrying across the asphalt, she cracked the closet door another inch. Koda's ears went up and his dark eyes widened in an I-don't-think-so stare.

"I'm not going out there," she said to the alert K-9. "I need to see and hear better."

Koda didn't move and his stare meant business.

"Good on you," she mumbled, her heart still crashing like a rockslide. "I don't know what to do."

She heard shots and put a hand to her mouth. She'd never felt so helpless. Well, maybe when Mack had become so aggressive and confrontational. But she'd managed to get out of that situation. Hadn't she?

"Please don't let it be him," she said. "Please."

Then she heard the back door open. Koda's ears lifted, and the big dog seemed to relax. Gavin?

"Sydney?"

"I'm still here, where you left me," she said on a sigh of relief. But her whole body trembled with the kind of jitters she usually got watching a horror movie.

"Koda, come." Gavin entered the room, and the dog woofed a low hello and hurried to his side. "Stay."

Gavin moved toward Sydney while Koda did as he'd commanded. He lifted her up and pulled her out of the closet.

"Are you all right?" he asked, his hands gentle on her arms.

"I'm fine, just imagining all kinds of bad scenarios," she replied. "How about you?"

"I'm okay. He got away."

"I heard shots."

"Yeah. He tried to shoot me, and I shot back. Called it in. Help's on the way. Apparently, he tried to use the trash can to get access to the laundry closet window. But he made enough noise to alert the whole neighborhood. I've seen bears do better at handling trash cans than this guy."

"It's not funny."

"I'm not laughing."

"So what do we do now?" she asked, so tired she could barely stand. "I'm sure the neighbors are wondering."

"The neighbors know what I do for a living, and I shooed in the ones who popped out back."

"Do I need to speak to your backup?"

"You're going to get some sleep," he said, dropping his hands away.

Sydney had been fully aware of the warmth of those hands or the strength he presented. "I am tired, but I don't think I'll sleep at all."

"Go and try," he said. "I'll handle the backup. I gave Dispatch a description, but it's murky. Dressed in dark clothing and a long dark bandana over his face. But I'm pretty sure he left some impressive footprints in the snow."

"That's good." She crossed her arms and rubbed her elbows. "I'll try to rest. But, Gavin, will you let me know if they find him?"

"Of course," he said. "And while you sleep, I'll do a search of your ex-boyfriend. If he's involved with this renegade group, we'll find him, too."

"Do you think that could have been Mack out there?"

"I don't know. If he's the way you describe him, and he's a member or leader of this group, then he'd send a minion to do the job. That was the first mistake. I don't think any of them will want to make another one."

"He knows how to hide," she said, a shiver crawling like a spider down her backbone. "A real survivalist type."

"I know how to find that kind of person," Gavin said, turning her toward the bathroom. "I put out clean towels and an old oversize T-shirt I got after running a five-K race. Rest up and we'll figure this out tomorrow."

"Thanks." She didn't know how to act or feel. This nightmare played in her head like a bad dream, where the good guy worked to save the world.

That good guy told his dog to stay, because right now he was trying to save her. Sydney would forever be thankful that Gavin had been taking a walk around the compound with Koda tonight. She couldn't, and wouldn't, think beyond that.

Koda found his bed and did a circle to get comfortable.

Sydney wished she could turn a circle and a find a peaceful spot to lay her head. Then she picked up the old T-shirt and held it close. It smelled clean and fresh and spicy.

And reminded her of Gavin.

SEVEN

Gavin sat on the small square front porch while Tyson Wilkes and his K-9 partner, Echo, stood on the walkway. Both were serious about their jobs.

"We got the footprints," Tyson, the leader of the RMKU, said. "That's something at least."

Tyson and Gavin went way back, having served together as army rangers in the Middle East. One day an operation had gone bad, and the team rescued a local Australian shepherd whose bark had saved them on a previous mission, but at the cost of a fellow soldier's life.

Echo. An amazingly brave animal trained in drug detection. Tyson had brought Echo home with him. But they'd gone through a rough year that almost shut down the whole RMKU and threatened Tyson's career. A brother of the only member of their unit who'd died that day had tried to get revenge on Tyson by sabotaging the RMKU and coming after him. Now, Tyson was engaged to be married to Skylar Morgan. A seasoned police detective, Skylar had helped Tyson solve that case, and would soon be in training to become a K-9 officer.

"See if they match the ones we got at the back door of the training yard office," Gavin said. "Two different people, but if they're serious outdoorsmen, there's a good chance they might buy and wear the same kind of boots. Samuels would want to fit in."

"As in military-type boots?" Tyson asked, glancing around. "I'll get the lab to do a comparison."

Things had calmed down now, but this place has been buzzing with officers and onlookers earlier.

"Yes." He told Tyson about the MSA and how they were probably behind this since Rick Samuels had possibly been deep inside their organization. "I don't know what they're up to, but we have to keep our eyes on them and find out. It's possible a man named Mack Creston is involved." He explained about Sydney's ex. "Doc Sydney is a target, and this is the second attempt tonight."

"Wow, we know how a man like that can snap. I'm glad you were on the scene." Then he checked his watch. "It's tomorrow. Three in the morning. You need to rest."

"And you need to get back to your vacation so you and Skylar can plan that wedding. I'm happy for you, brother."

Tyson grinned. "I'm happy for me, too. But you know if you need me I'll be in town throughout the holidays. Skylar and I can help with research, too."

"Thanks," Gavin said. "I appreciate that."

Given that they'd both suffered PTSD from their ranger years, Gavin was thankful to be back with his friend. It was hard to stop the nightmares, but good to know time healed a lot of wounds.

"Okay, you've got a patrol watching. Go and get some shuteye," Tyson said.

"Sleep on demand, sleep when you can," Gavin said, remembering their ranger days and Tyson repeating one of his favorite phrases over and over.

"Don't you know it, man."

After Tyson and Echo left, Gavin did one last check. An end unit with another building a few feet to the right. Anyone could hide anywhere around here. Even in an empty apartment.

The uneasiness he'd felt since seeing Rick Samuels holding a gun on Sydney wouldn't go away until he could apprehend her tormenters. So he went inside and made a cup of coffee and turned on his laptop.

He'd call SAC Bridges first thing and request to be cleared and read in on the MSA files the FBI already had. He hoped they wouldn't take him off the case and go all FBI on him, since technically Samuels had been working for them.

Because he didn't plan to let Sydney out of his sight until she could feel safe again.

Sydney woke with a start, her mind reeling with the nightmare of a man holding a gun on her.

Koda barked aggressively and then the bedroom door flew up. Gavin stood there with his gun drawn.

"What's wrong?" she said, sitting up, her hand ruffling her hair.

"You screamed." Gavin rushed to the windows and checked the closet, Koda on his heels.

"I—I had a bad dream." She grabbed her lab coat and dragged it over the long T-shirt. "The man, the gun. I'm okay."

Gavin stood there, barefoot, wearing an old shirt and jeans.

Better than her dream. Much better.

"I thought—"

"No one is here, Gavin. But thank you. And you, too, Koda."

Koda woofed a low thanks while Gavin continued staring at her. "You're all right."

"I just need…coffee. Lots of coffee."

Gavin let out a huff. "Of course."

"What time is it?"

"Seven a.m."

"I need to get to my veterinary practice. I didn't get a chance to alert my staff last night."

"I'll take you."

She shooed him out and got dressed. She'd been way too distracted and now she worried about the people she worked with. It had all blurred in her brain and turned into that awful dream.

Determined to end this nightmare, Sydney would find out the truth about Mack. Then she'd get new alarms for her home and the clinic. And she'd take her handgun to work with her. She had a permit, and she knew how to use that gun.

"Boy, am I glad to see you."

Sydney hurried around the waiting-room counter. Her assistant, Jennifer Baker, was standing at the door to the office, her eyes wide. "I heard you were attacked last night."

"I'm okay," Sydney said, surprised at how fast word could get around these days. "Sorry I overslept."

Jennifer's blue eyes grew two sizes. "If you're okay, why is that hunk and his highly alert K-9 shadowing you."

Sydney glanced outside. "Well, that's a long story. Is everything okay here?"

Jennifer shrugged. "The few animals we're boarding were fidgety this morning, but we're okay." She turned to the small kitchen around the corner from the counter. "I can tell you need coffee."

"Lots of it," Sydney said. She tugged at her always tousled hair and remembered the nightmare she'd been living since last night. "So no patients this morning?"

"Not yet, but our clients probably saw the same news flash I saw. Maybe they're giving you some space."

Sydney inhaled a long sip of coffee. "Misinformation

can ruin a good business. I'll talk to Gavin about putting out an official report. I don't need bad publicity."

"Oh, it's not all bad," Jennifer said. "The phone's been ringing with calls from concerned clients."

As if on cue, the phone did start ringing. "You'd better get that then," Sydney said. Then she turned to look outside.

Gavin and Koda came around the corner and pushed open the front door. "Everything okay in here?" he asked.

"Yes," she said. "But I haven't searched every corner yet."

"We'll handle that," he said. Then he leaned in, his voice low. "Footprints all around the back door. But they didn't make it inside. Just go about your business while we do a check."

"Right."

Sydney stared after him while Jennifer took care of the phone calls.

"That was strange," Jennifer said, her blond bangs slipping over her eyes. "The man on the phone said to tell you he'd see you soon."

Sydney's stomach roiled, the coffee she'd drunk turning sour. "Did he leave a name?"

"No," Jennifer replied. "He wanted you to know that. Should I be worried?"

"No," Sydney said. She wouldn't scare Jennifer yet, but she'd have to let Gavin know about this.

She had a strong feeling Mack Creston had just called. Because that's what he'd said to her the last time they'd talked in person.

EIGHT

Gavin didn't like this.

They'd compared the boot prints from the K-9 building, his apartment and now the clinic. They all matched a certain kind of boot—Terrain XX. The lab had gone over all of them and compared the treads. He'd scanned the files on MSA last night and learned the once great organization had fallen into bad hands after the last living son of the founder had died. Apparently, *his* rogue son had inherited the family money and status within the foundation. A lot of upstanding members had left.

But the private group required sponsored memberships. That meant Rick Samuels had managed to convince someone to sponsor him and get him inside. Gavin hadn't been able to find any connections or a member list. But based on Bridges' files, they were in deep with illegal drugs and firearms.

So that left him trying to find places in Denver and all of Colorado that might carry Terrain XX tactical boots so they could pull up video footage and sales receipts. A long shot, but a start.

One man dead and others trying to get to Sydney. Someone had shown up at her clinic, but there could be several out there, looking and waiting. Gavin was fully prepared to guard Sydney, but how long could they go on like this?

For now, he'd do what he had to do. He'd been through worse.

After they'd checked her animals at her cabin, Gavin sat in the clinic all day, Koda at his feet. They'd only had a few clients today. A sick cat named PJ had hissed a daring greeting to Koda. The K-9 ignored the cat, his training hard-core and strong. Followed by a beautiful osprey with a damaged wing, and a Chihuahua named Bruiser that had a bad attitude and barked his way through his exam and then snarled at everyone and sniffed his little nose at Koda as he shot by. The Malinois almost did an eyeroll on that one.

They'd ordered in lunch, so Gavin got to see Sydney interact with her staff and reassure them they were safe.

But Gavin worried that her two assistants, Jennifer Baker and a senior citizen named Robert Whitson, might not be safe. He'd explained what he could to both of them.

"My husband has a big gun collection," Jennifer had told him. "And our place has alarms everywhere."

"I'll watch out," Robert said. "I'd do anything for Doc Sydney. She gave me a job when everyone else thought I was washed up."

Neither of them could imagine anyone wanting to harm Sydney.

Gavin couldn't imagine that, either. Sydney was good with her people and single-minded when it came to animals. She'd walked him around her acre of property and introduced him to all of her own animals this morning. A roan named Herman, a mean goat she called GOAT—the greatest of all time—a feisty cat named Rocky and a fussy parrot named Repeat who called out "hey, Doc," every time she entered the room. Apparently, the parrot liked to interrupt any conversation and could mimic people.

Her cabin wasn't far from town, but it was isolated.

"My neighbor, Roscoe Kendrick, is a retired widower.

I send him sweet treats and he feeds and takes care of the animals when I'm working nights at the lab."

"Can you trust him?"

"Of course, and he loves doing it. Says it keeps him from being so lonely."

Sydney made other people feel special. Gavin had noticed that about her many times over. He figured that's why she'd probably tried to make things work with Mack Creston, but some people never saw kindness through a haze of anger. He could have easily been one of those people after coming home from his last tour.

Now he was glad he'd made it here to help Sydney.

After the day went with no disruptions, he helped her lock up. Someone else had been put in charge of the two kenneled dogs back at RMKU. SAC Bridges had called once to check in.

"We can't place Mack Creston as a member yet, but I've got people on that. I sent two agents out to some of the big outdoor stores to gather receipts and video recordings on anyone buying Terrain XX boots."

Gavin needed to update Sydney. He'd watched her work all day without complaint, while he did some searches of his own.

"You're amazing," he said once they were in his SUV and on the way to her house. "You went through the worst last night, and today, you smiled and assured frantic pet owners things would be okay. How do you do that, Doc?"

She shook her head. "The same way you do your job, Gavin. I take it minute by minute, hour by hour, day by day. And I pray through every hour, trust me."

"Tell me about you and this Mack person. I need a profile on him. Do you know the last place he lived?"

"He didn't live with me if that's what you're asking. And I never went to his apartment. He always came to pick me up at my place or at the clinic. He claimed his place was too full of outdoor stuff."

"Were you ever curious?"

Sydney shuddered in her seat. "Of course, but he'd laugh my questions off, and he was the grand-gesture type— flowers, chocolates, a new jacket or sweater. He dazzled and distracted me. We were only together a few months. He found a cheap apartment nearby, but he left there after we broke up."

"I know," Gavin said. "No evidence, and no one there remembers him. He's leaving the land how he found it."

She shook her head. "I should have been more curious, but I didn't want to be clingy. We hadn't been dating that long before things went wrong. Mack has certain notions about women, and my working all the time didn't help matters. I love my work and I couldn't give it up just to please him. So now I'm gun-shy about relationships."

"I understand that," he said, "But this one sounds like the overprotective type."

"Yes, so be careful, Gavin. Mack's serious about his tough-guy image."

Gavin tilted his head. "You're a friend, and you're in danger. And I come highly trained with the finest K-9 partner."

"Koda is the best," she said, giving the dog in the back a smile. Koda gave her a soft woof in return. "And here I thought you two were hanging around because of my charm and wit."

"You're too serious to use that sharp wit. But I like that about you, too. You do get in your zingers."

"I have a small funny bone." Then she sighed. "I used to use humor to hide my pain. A big dysfunctional family can bring out either the best or the worst in a person. Humor and grace are my fallback tactics."

"I get that," he admitted. "Tyson and I saw a lot of

things being rangers. We had to become hard-nosed and sarcastic, or we'd have never survived. We barely survived, anyway, after that horrible explosion."

"You've been a good friend to him, Gavin."

"Tyson and I go way back."

Sydney smiled at that. "You're that kind of man. The kind who's loyal and kind and caring. I like that about you."

He wanted to tell her he thought a lot of her, too. She had the whole cute-package thing down. Pretty, quiet until she wasn't, serious until she smiled and the kind of woman a man only wished he could find.

And here she was, forced to be around him all day. A man who'd seen too much death and lived a thousand battles, and not just military battles. He didn't think he had the heart for romance and marriage. Or a family.

But if he did…

"I hope you're taking this threat seriously," he said, getting back to business as they turned onto the rocky road to her place.

"I've thought about it most of last night, and all day today." She pushed at her gamine bangs. "You might think I'm professional and I try to be, but today I had to stop and remember to breathe. I didn't know Rick Samuels, but I'm thankful he told the truth before he died. I only wish he could have given us more information."

"Yeah, me, too," Gavin said. "We're trying to match the boot treads so we can narrow down the suspects, but that's like looking for a needle in a haystack. This might take a while."

"Don't worry. I'm tough." But her words were diminished by the wariness in her expression.

"I know you're tough," he said, wishing he could crack her thick skin, "but it's Christmas. You can take some time—the time you'd already planned to take. What does that involve?"

"I'd get any patients settled. Jennifer keeps things going. And the K-9 kennel dogs have helpers to watch out for them. Shiloh and Cleo right now. Jodie or Skylar will make rounds."

Shiloh, the black Lab, hadn't worked out as a possible recruit for the K-9 unit. But Tyson's assistant, Jodie Chen, had seen how he'd quickly adapted to silent signals. Having a deaf mother, Jodie had learned sign language and she believed Shiloh would make a great service dog.

"Okay, once we get that worked out, you can hunker down."

"Where, Gavin?" she asked as he parked and scanned the surrounding rocky terrain and woods. "Where should I hunker down? Here? Or back at your place? Maybe I should go to Kansas and visit my family."

"Wherever you are, I'll be with you until we figure this out," he said. "Do you trust me, Doc?"

"I do," she said, her dark eyes sincere. "But you don't need to be responsible for me all the time."

"Look, Sydney," he said, turning to face her, "I'm the one who found you with Rick Samuels, so now I'm sticking to you, okay? I really didn't have any big holiday plans."

"Oh, I see." She got out of the SUV and met him and Koda in front of the big vehicle. "So I'm the best you've got?"

Back to sarcasm again.

"You are the best," he said, meaning it, feeling it, as he stared at her. She was a kind, decent human being—a coworker. But that wild hair and her dark eyes held him and made him want to protect her.

Would she let him do that?

NINE

They went to her place to check in on the animals again. The property was set against a rocky hilltop leading up toward the mountains. Gavin sent Koda in first and followed, Sydney holding one hand on his shoulder to stick with him.

Repeat, the vivid blue-and-yellow-feathered parrot, whistled from his cage in the corner. "K-9, K-9!"

"How does he know that?" Gavin whispered.

"He hears me on the phone talking about K-9s all the time, and I've brought a few dogs here to recover when their owners needed help. I call them my canines, so he picked it up that way."

"Ah." They moved down the hallway and met Rocky. The big black-and-white spotted cat shot out of sight like a flying ball of fur.

"Rocky is antihuman," she explained. "But he likes dogs."

Koda sniffed, his nose high in the air.

"Your horse and goat are a bit more friendly, thankfully," Gavin said after they'd checked the bedrooms.

"I have to make sure they're warm and safe."

Gavin nodded, his expression serious and focused. Determined. Koda followed suit. Sydney held on to his heavy nylon jacket.

"All clear," he said, pivoting close after searching the garage. "Nothing out of order, no one in the closets."

Sydney took her hand from his shoulder only to have him right there. So close, she could see the unique light blue color of his eyes, could see the traces of laugh lines mixed with fatigue circling them. "I'm glad you two are here with me."

Gavin held her for a moment, then stepped away. "So you agree this is the plan—you, me and Koda, spending time together?"

Sydney gave that some thought because she sensed the doubt in his words. "That's not a bad way to start the holidays, but I'm sorry about this."

"Don't be sorry. We want to keep our vet alive."

"Of course." She wouldn't get caught up in these emotions pouring over her like a snowdrift shedding icicles. Gavin was doing a job, protecting a coworker. Nothing else.

"Doc?"

"Hmmm?"

"*Are* you sure about this?"

"Yes." She put on her blank face. "I never expected anything like this to happen. The RMKU takes care of so many people in trouble, and you go after the people causing trouble. I'm just the animal doctor in this equation. A sideline, a shadow person, there when I'm needed. Now I'm in the thick of things."

"You are more than what you just mentioned," Gavin said, leaning back against her small kitchen counter. "We, the team…we need you. So no more apologizing. It's only a few weeks until Christmas. Let's pretend you invited Koda and me over for dinner. Okay?"

"Okay." Sydney had never thought of Gavin in that way—as in the inviting-over-to-dinner way. But now she was fully aware of how his strength and presence filled her tiny cabin. She had to admit, he made her feel safe. "I'll see what I can actually make for dinner."

"I'll help," he said, turning to take in her living room, his gaze hitting on the small blue puffy sofa Rocky loved to curl up on, and the big lush beige chair and ottoman where Sydney read books and drank coffee on her off time. Repeat sat in his huge wire cage by the window, his hooded gaze on the furry animal staring at him. "Uh, Doc, we have a big problem."

"What?" Sydney asked, her heart trembling as she searched the entire room.

"You don't have a Christmas tree."

She breathed in relief. "I haven't had time to decorate or get a tree, same as you since you didn't have one, either."

"Well, we have to remedy that," Gavin said with a sheepish smile. "First thing tomorrow, we'll find a tree. We'll have to sneak to do it, of course. A covert Christmas operation, but at least we have a goal."

"Of course." She grinned, glad they could focus on something positive. "I have a few decorations in the garage."

Gavin came around the counter to where she was standing. "What have you got to cook?"

She opened the narrow pantry by the refrigerator. "I like homemade pizza," she said. "I don't make the crust, but the ones I buy ready-made are pretty good. I have veggies and…hmmm, veggies. Do you mind not having a fully loaded meat pizza?"

"Veggies?" Gavin glanced at Koda, horror in both their eyes. "I think I can live with that." Then he pointed a finger hidden behind his other hand. "But Koda, not so much. Good thing I only feed him once a day and give him a *t-r-e-a-t* vitamin at dinnertime."

Koda's ears lifted. Did the dog know how to spell *treat*?

"I'll go change out of these clothes I've had on over

twenty-four hours. You can grab the pizza crusts and get the two round pans out from under the stove. I'll be right back."

"We're on it, right, Koda?"

Koda woofed and Rocky came charging by, sniffing and hissing. Koda didn't even bat an eye.

"Good boy," Gavin and Sydney both said at the same time.

She laughed as she entered the bedroom and grabbed a quick shower. Maybe she'd be safe here for at least one night.

A short time later, she walked out into the hallway, her hair damp and her feet bare, and she heard a crash, followed by Koda's fierce bark.

"Sydney, get down."

Sydney dived to the hallway floor. Rocky came up to rub against her. Repeat went wild, squawking and flapping his wings.

"All clear," Gavin called out from the direction of the kitchen.

"All clear," Repeat mimicked.

Koda came down the hallway, Gavin hurrying along with the K-9.

"What happened?" she asked after Gavin helped her up.

"Someone threw a rock at the kitchen window," Gavin explained. "I'd bent down to get the pizza pans when it happened. If you'd been standing there, the rock could have hit you in the head, Sydney."

Sydney slumped against the hallway wall. "Did the rock have a message?"

Gavin nodded, his eyes dark with rage, his jaw muscles tensing up. "Yes. Written in black—'I'll see you soon.'"

Sydney nodded, closed her eyes. "Gavin, that's what

Mack told me the last time I saw him—after we'd broken up."

"So you got a phone message at the clinic and now a rock thrown into your house, both with those same words."

"Mack is not done with me yet."

"Mack has messed with the wrong people, Sydney."

"He isn't going to give up. He likes to win."

"Well, so do we, remember," Gavin said. "We like to get the bad guys off the streets." He touched his hand to her arm. "You go and get that gun you told me about and stay in your room with the door locked. Koda and I are going to go out and check around."

She nodded and quickly returned with a loaded Glock, knowing not to argue with him. But her heart now held a new fear. What if something happened to Gavin while he was protecting her? How could she ever live with that?

TEN

Gavin and Koda walked around the property, Gavin holding a flashlight under his weapon, Koda taking the lead. The K-9 guided Gavin to the small barn that held one horse stall and a corner stall for the big goat, with another barn door to the round corral behind the building.

"Let's see what we've got," Gavin said, commanding Koda to search.

The Malinois took off and held his nose to the ground then lifted it in the air. Then he headed toward the back of the barn, where another set of doors opened to a rocky hilltop.

Koda went on alert at the doors, going still while he glanced back at Gavin. Gavin slipped through the stable alley, careful not to hit the mountain bike in the corner, or the haystack up against the wall. He noticed footprints on the dirt floor—heavy boot prints with a thick tread, a familiar tread.

The door lock had been broken, causing one side to hit against the other with a sinister *tap, tap, tap* as the wind howled down the rocky hillside. Gavin slid to the side and glanced at Koda. The dog stayed on alert.

Gavin lifted his hand to give the go command, then kicked the door open and prepared to shoot.

Koda barked his way toward the rocky outcroppings,

then tried to find a path up. He made it the top of the ridge and stopped.

Gavin followed, realizing that someone had run up this hilltop, but they could be hiding down in one of the crevasses on the other side. After calling Koda back, Gavin did the same. He settled against a rocky face and listened. Koda stood silent.

Then Gavin heard it. The soft crackling of boots hitting rocks. Someone had been here, no doubt. But why?

He heard a gunshot from the cabin, causing his pulse to go full throttle and his heart to chase after it.

Sydney. They'd planned this so they could get to Sydney.

"Go," he called to Koda.

The dog barked and followed Gavin, galloping at top speed toward the house. As they approached, another shot boomed into the night, echoing over the yard. Inside, Gavin could hear the parrot ranting and squawking again. The bird was good at alerting.

Gavin knew better than to let Sydney out of his sight. Fearing the worst, he banged open the front door and searched for Sydney, his head filling with all kinds of dread.

"Doc?"

Koda woofed toward the kitchen. Gavin said a prayer as he rounded the corner of the island.

And found Sydney sitting there with her weapon drawn toward the busted window. She didn't move. "They tried to get into my bedroom window. I came out and shot at someone on my porch."

"So I heard," he said, dropping down beside her. "Sydney, give me the gun."

She finally blinked and glanced around. "Okay." Handing over her weapon, she asked, "So what did you find in the barn?"

Gavin took her hand, checked her pupils. She was way too calm for what had just happened. "Someone was there, but they ran off into the foothills. I'm sorry."

"It's okay," she said. "Mine got away, too. But Gavin, I'm pretty sure I injured him."

Gavin called in a report and let Bridges know about a possible gunshot victim roaming the area. The SAC said they'd check all the local hospitals. He also told Gavin they had several matches for local outdoors stores that sold Terrain XX boots. "Military-grade, just as we thought. I'll send you the list."

"And I'll makes some calls," Gavin told Bridges. "Also, Sydney feels certain her ex, Mack Creston, is behind this." He told Bridges about the message on the rock and the cryptic phone call at her clinic. "He's harassing her and threatening her, or someone who works for him is doing so."

"We'll stay on it," Bridges said. "But I doubt we'll find anyone shot. They'll go to ground."

After thanking SAC Bridges, Gavin knew he'd have a long night ahead of him.

Now, however, he wanted to check on Sydney. After he'd taped up the broken window with a temporary piece of heavy plastic, he'd checked on Repeat then covered the excited bird's cage. Sydney had gone back to preparing pizza. Her way of coping, he supposed.

"That smells good," he said after he'd done the rounds. He knew a patrol car was sitting at the entrance to her place now, but even that precaution didn't calm his fears. These people, whoever they were, seemed to blend in with the countryside and probably had come here on foot through the mountains.

"It should be ready in ten minutes," she said. She got ice and poured them both a soda, then checked the oven again.

Gavin waited until she stood up straight and then gave her a long stare. "Hey, are you okay?"

"Why wouldn't I be?" she asked. "I mean, in the last twenty-four hours, I've been held at gunpoint by a man who got killed in the hospital, stalked at your place, had someone trespassing on my property and I've possibly wounded someone else. Not to mention, you're here guarding me and how that's disrupted both our lives, and all because I broke up with a sociopath who thinks women are beneath him in every possible way." Throwing down her animal-embossed potholder, she asked, "Why wouldn't I be okay?"

"Sydney," he said, taking her by her arms to stop her from pacing, "it's okay to have a meltdown. I'd say you're due one."

"I told you I don't have meltdowns."

"I know, but we all do at times."

"Not you. You're as cool as…a mountain stream."

He smiled at that. "Cold, you mean?"

"I didn't say that. You do your job in a professional manner."

"This is more than a job now," he admitted. "This is dangerous and you're my friend. I can't let anyone harm you or hurt you in any way. I have to help you."

"That's what I mean. You always do the right thing."

"Yes, I try, but this time it's about more than that. I'm sworn to carry out the law, and that means I have to do my best and try to keep my emotions and anger under control."

"You're good at that."

"And so are you," he said, noting the mist in her eyes. "You handled Rick Samuels like a pro and found a way to save yourself. I'm guessing you were the one in your chaotic family who had to maintain a tight control, to deal with the fallout, to keep things running smoothly. Am I correct?"

Her armor slipped. She pushed him away. "I did what I had to do, growing up. My parents weren't the best at staying calm or organized. I guess because of that I'm always trying to keep things under control, including myself and my reactions to the world. Mack…didn't understand that concept. He did everything in his power to push all my buttons. And finally, I'd had enough."

"So you lost it with him?" Gavin asked, needing to know she would be okay.

"I didn't really lose it, so to speak. I told him I'd had enough of him trying to control my life, including everything from what I wore, to how I lived—church and family—to my job. You name it, Mack was against it. He wanted a submissive type, and he thought if he married me, he could make me bend to his rules since he gave me elaborate gifts and knew what was best for me. I'd quit work and I'd take care of the household and…our children." She shrugged. "Don't get me wrong—I want those things one day, but not with a man who expects way more than I'm willing to give."

Gavin wanted to slap the man's head. "I'm sorry, Sydney. I had no idea. None of us had any way of knowing what you'd been through."

"I didn't want anyone to know," she said, her voice rising. "And I'm so angry now, I could… I could…do something I'd regret."

The oven buzzer went off, causing her to step back. Gavin took her potholder and got the pizza out of the oven, then placed it on the stove. When he turned back, she was standing there with her hands gripping the counter, her knuckles pale, her head down.

"I'm so angry," she finally whispered. "I wanted to start fresh, and I got the loan to buy the clinic. I poured my heart into that place and this tiny cabin. I wanted to be left alone, to be me. I decided marriage was out of the question for me. I seem to attract the wrong kind of man."

"No," Gavin said, pulling her around. "Doc, listen to me. You are not the problem here. Mack Creston is. He's the kind of man no one likes, someone who thinks he's above reproach, that he can get away with anything because he has power. He's the worst kind of criminal, because in his head he believes he knows best and he's doing what's right. But he is so wrong."

Sydney finally looked up and into his eyes. Gavin saw the pain, the shame, the longing in her gaze. "Sydney, you are better than him, better than whatever he said to make you feel less than. Don't let this attack make you think any differently, okay?" He touched a hand to her cheek. "He's gone way too far this time. He's decided if he can't have you, no one can. And that's about as dangerous as a man can get."

She nodded and then, the meltdown came. Tears rolled down her cheeks while she held her lips tightly together. Forgetting all the rules, Gavin pulled her close and then walked her to the couch. They sat down and he tugged her into his arms and held her there.

"Let it all out," he said. "It's okay. It's just you, me and Koda. No one will have to know."

Koda came and sat by Sydney, and then after a nod from Gavin, placed his nose on her knee. Which made tough, controlled Doc Sydney cry even more.

Gavin held her, his arms around her, Koda at her feet, the dog's big eyes on her. "We've got you, Doc. We've got you."

Sydney sighed and sniffed and held tight, while Gavin lost his heart.

ELEVEN

Sydney woke to find the sun streaming into the bedroom window. It took her a moment, but soon the events of the night came pouring over her, along with the early morning sunshine.

Trying to block out the horror, she instead thought about Gavin and how he'd held her and let her cry. No one had ever done that with her before. Her large, loud family discouraged any show of emotions, and her older brothers and sisters had been too caught up in their own lives to notice Sydney. So she'd turned to animals because they honed in on her anxieties and doubts.

Mack had scoffed at any sign of tears. He didn't like her menagerie of animals, either. Called them a nuisance and too much responsibility. Comparing that to how Gavin fed her animals and talked to them to calm them down, she decided to focus on Gavin and Koda, her protectors, and she'd keep finding ways to protect herself. Just as she always had. Especially with her emotions.

She got up, washed her face and brushed her teeth, then pulled on a pair of jeans, boots and a long sweater.

When she went into the kitchen, she found Koda by the door. More like in front of the door. But Gavin was nowhere to be seen.

"Where did he go?" she asked Koda, her mind racing

with bad images. He'd still been up searching for leads when she'd finally gone to bed. "Tell me he's safe, Koda."

Koda woofed a calm response.

"So he's out there and he left you in here to watch over me?"

Another soft woof.

"I see."

She took the cover off Repeat's cage. "I see," Repeat said immediately, fussing and cawing at the big dog. "I see."

"You do see everything," Sydney said, remembering when she'd bought the parrot to keep her company. Repeat and Rocky were both sources of entertainment and good distractions.

Rocky sprinted by, as if being called, ready for his breakfast. Koda gave the cat a side-eye stare but maintained his working position.

If she knew Gavin, and she was getting to know him even more, she figured he'd be checking everything again in the light of day. She'd been so upset that someone had been in the barn, but he'd assured her GOAT and Herman were okay.

So what would he find out there this morning?

She would soon have her answer. Gavin had locked the front door behind him, and now knocked and waved through the window.

After she opened the door, he came in carrying a four-foot-tall Colorado blue spruce. A tree. The man had gone out and found a tree.

While she smiled and put her hands to her face, she also noticed the patrol SUV sitting at the end of her driveway.

"You went out for a tree?"

"I went out to see if I could find any evidence of your shooting skills, and I didn't. I stumbled on this little beauty, so I thought we could take our minds off this case for a while and decorate. I mean, I didn't have a tree at my place, and you don't have one here. This, we can do."

She nodded and made coffee and buttered some bread for toast, then grabbed the blueberry jelly she'd made during the summer when her life had been perfectly mundane. She wanted that again.

"Thank you," she said after they sat down for breakfast. Koda had his one meal of the day and Repeat busily ate his pellets and a banana.

"Thank you," Repeat mimicked.

Gavin took a bite of toast and jelly. "This is good. You made the jelly?"

"I did," she said. "I grew up on a farm, so my sisters and I learned to freeze, jar and can every kind of fruit and vegetable."

He smiled at her. "That's nice, to still have those memories."

"I do have some good memories from my childhood," she said. "My parents were hard-working but now they're retired. They about worked themselves to death before we could convince them to slow down."

"Farming is hard work."

"Yes." She nibbled her toast, her stomach still roiling with worry and dread. "So no bodies out there, not even any blood?"

"No. I think you scared your intruder off." He put down his coffee cup. "I found a few more tracks, which I've marked so the crime-scene techs can plaster them. I also checked with several big-box outdoor stores, and they'll go back to check receipts on Terrain XX boots. Most of them agree the boots are expensive and they only carry a few of the styles. The receipts will show what kind of boots were bought, and if we need a warrant to get names and faces, we can take care of that."

"Progress, but still no humans found, dead or alive."

"No, not yet. No reports of gunshot wounds in any of the area hospitals, but I'm thinking if you made a mark they'd get their man back to the camp and take care of him there."

"But we still don't know where the main MSA camp is located."

"Working on that, but we can't find anything to pin on these people. We need to find Mack Creston." He rubbed his tired eyes. "I studied up on the organization last night, but privacy is high maintenance and MSA tends to move around, so I didn't learn much else than what we already know. The location is a secret. In the high country. Samuels didn't leave many details on how to get there, but we're still searching his last known address. Do you know how Mack got in?"

"Someone who vouched for him," she said. "He didn't talk about it much. But he went on long trips, acting as a scout, or so he told me. He always had ready cash, I can tell you that."

"They're up to no good," Gavin replied. "That's what we need to prove. Samuels worked hard on that angle, but he had to prove himself."

"Which is what they wanted. They wanted him to kill me and then they'd kill him, eliminating two people in one hit."

"Him, I get," Gavin said. "You, I don't understand. You've done nothing to hurt MSA, and as much as I'd like to close them down, why would this group that likes to stay secret and hidden encourage Creston to come after you?"

"I can think of one reason," she said. "Mack would not like me working for the locals, and he'd make that clear as a threat to the group. That could win him points and fuel his big ego. Especially if he found out about the regional K-9 unit here to assist the FBI with cases—a team I now work for part-time. He'd be angry, and it's a perfect excuse to make sure I get what I deserve, according to him. And to up his status within the organization."

"He'd convince them that you're working with the very law-enforcement agency trying to shut down the MSA, right?"

"Right," she said, pushing away her toast. "It's a personal insult to him—that and me leaving him, of course. He wants me to pay, and now he has a way to get that done. This group doesn't follow the rules, from what I've heard."

"Like I said, the kind of dangerous we don't need. Reckless and out for revenge, irrational and unreasonable."

Sydney got up to put away their dishes. "He won't stop. He's found me now, but I wasn't trying to hide. That's my mistake. I thought he'd moved on."

"He's obviously been watching you, biding his time and waiting for the best time."

"Christmas," she said. "He never did like the holidays."

"He's a real grinch. If he's gone rogue and hired a few underlings to do some of the dirty work, that's a whole other thing. I'm waiting to hear what the techs find at Rick Samuels's last known address. Might shed some light on where this camp is located, and where Creston is, too."

Gavin refilled his coffee cup. "Meantime, we're gonna decorate this tree. Then we'll send out for groceries, and I'm adding meat to that list."

"I'm sorry."

"Good pizza, but you hardly ate any."

She felt a blush rising up her cheeks. "I—I was busy having that meltdown you suggested."

She was busy right now remembering being in his arms, but Sydney wasn't ready for a romantic relationship. Mack had never laid a hand on her, but he'd left his mark on her. She was afraid to let go and try again, even with a man who'd shown her so many things that made him different from the rest. Gavin was the opposite of Mack—a good, decent, hardworking officer who'd also served in the military. Mack played at being some kind of tough guy, while Gavin lived the reality of that.

Gavin was doing his job and they'd both gotten caught up in an emotional tangle last night. She had to make sure that didn't happen again, because she couldn't risk losing a good friend who might not want more than a working relationship.

TWELVE

Gavin set up the tree in the small stand she'd found. Now they were unraveling lights and finding ornaments, most of which were animals in campy Christmas attire. Dogs wearing little red-and-green sweaters, cats wearing red hats, horses with bright saddles and birds, of course, one with Santa at the ocean, a seagull sitting on Rudolph's antlers.

He glanced over at Sydney, glad her mood had improved. The crime techs had come and gone, so hopefully they'd get some prints from the barn and off the rock that had been thrown through the window. He'd patched that up with some old glass until they could get a new pane in.

He had the electronic files on Rick Samuels to go over and was waiting to hear from Bridges on any new information on the MSA. So tree decorating it was for the next hour or so at least.

"More coffee?" she asked as she came back into the living room. Sydney had checked in at the clinic and Tyson had done rounds in the kennels at the RMKU complex. Her staff had held down the fort at the clinic and the RMKU kennels were okay.

The local police force had eyes on both places, but that didn't mean much to these ruthless people. But it could make them think twice about trying to mess around at her office or the kennels again.

Of course, they obviously knew she lived here, but hopefully last night, Koda's barks and Sydney's bullets had scared them away.

"I'm good." Gavin still wasn't used to seeing Sydney in civilian clothes since she always wore a lab coat over her jeans and T-shirts at work. She was attractive, a real outdoors girl—woman—who knew her way around animals and guns. Her hair was different—short but touching her cheeks and neck, a messy, choppy style that kind of moved with the wind. She didn't fuss with it, and she wore the bare minimum of makeup on her porcelain skin.

Gavin had noticed her at the training center, but now he could see her. The real her underneath that carefully controlled veneer. He liked her. A lot.

"Are you stuck?" she asked, bringing him back to the moment. "You've been studying that string of lights for a while now."

"Uh, yeah, I think I've got it all figured out," he said, covering for what he'd really finally figured out. He had a big crush on the doc, the woman he'd vowed to protect.

This could get complicated since she acted gun-shy about another relationship.

"It's complicated," she said. "I've never found a good way to keep a cord of lights from untangling."

"Yeah, a real tangled mess," he said, referring to his feelings more than to the wad of lights wrapped across his fingers. "But I'll get it straightened out. And *yes* on the coffee."

She got them fresh refills and then helped him slowly unwind the cord of lights. "I haven't put up a tree in years. I usually go home, but this year I'd decided I'd stay here and explore my own backyard."

"Well, when this is all over I'd be happy to explore with you," he said. "I miss my family back in New Mexico, but Denver is growing on me. So much to do and see."

"Did you have a good childhood?" she asked, her eyes sincere.

"I did," he said, smiling. "My parents are traditional, and we hold certain Christmas traditions each year. But they're on a long-planned-out trip to Europe. My siblings and I each contributed to the trip, so they could travel in style. So no family Christmas this year since my brothers and their families are scattered to the wind and I'm here, and new to the RMKU at that. I offered to cover the holidays and now I'm glad I did."

Sydney held up the string of lights, stopping to stare at him. "I'm glad you did, too. I can't think beyond that, Gavin."

"Me, either," he said, not wanting to imagine how this could be so very different if he hadn't heard Shiloh barking. "My mother used to say God puts us where we need to be, and I guess this situation has proved that."

She didn't dispute him. "That's a nice thought." Giving him another shy smile, she said, "I'm glad it was you, Gavin."

He nodded, his own smile impossible to hide. "You have a crush on Koda, right? He's your favorite K-9."

Koda's ears perked up, and Repeat stared Gavin down from his lofty perch.

"Absolutely," she said with a grin.

"Absolutely," Repeat said, his eyes still on Gavin.

"Little ears hear big things," she whispered.

"Yes, they do." He'd have to be careful he didn't talk to himself, or her nosy bird might repeat everything he said out loud.

"So tell me about some of your traditions," she said, holding up the twisted string of bulbs to uncoil the electrical wire.

He started stringing the lights onto the tree. "Well, my

favorite is the *Navidad milagro* tree my mom puts up at Christmas."

He saw the questions in her eyes. "It's a small metal tree you set on a table, and you hang little metal ornaments on it—*milagro* means 'miracle' in Spanish. These are usually handmade or artisan symbols, some such as the heart to represent humans and animal shapes to represent nature and animals. All of them are to show thanks and ask for good favor and blessings from God." He stopped stringing the tiny lights and looked at one of the bulbs. "My mother told me the little miracles of life make a good life. We only need to know where to find them."

"I love that," she said. "It sounds beautiful."

"The one my family always displays has been passed down through the family. It's not only special. It's price-less to my *mamá*. My dad is not Hispanic, but he indulges her because he loves her so much."

"So that makes it priceless to you," she said, her gaze holding his, a longing in her eyes.

"I guess so." He hadn't stopped to think about how much he missed his family. His parents represented what he wanted in life—a strong love, and a strong family. "It's safely packed away for now. But next Christmas, I'm sure it will be on display on the buffet, where all the pies and cakes are also displayed."

Her gaze darkened, the look in her eyes faraway. "You and your family are obviously close. I can tell you miss them."

"I do, but hey, I'm okay. We're here and while things are scary right now, we'll see better days, Doc. Remember that."

"I'm trying," she said. "I know you'll do your best to protect me, but, Gavin, please be careful. Please."

"Always," he said. "Now let's get the ornaments on this tree so we can light her up!"

Sydney laughed at that. Rocky came flying toward the tree then skidded underneath. Repeat squawked, "Light her up!"

Gavin rolled his eyes and laughed. "Never a dull moment in this house." He just wished they weren't trying to stay one step ahead of a killer.

THIRTEEN

For a while, the tree sent away the gloom hanging over them. But Sydney's nerves were on high alert. Each time the wind blew, or the snow fell off the roof, she shivered and checked the fire. She hated the vulnerability of fear. It clawed at her soul and left a deep gash of doubt and apprehension, such as she'd never felt. Why did she feel so cold and scared?

Glancing out the one good pane left in the broken window, she knew the answer to that. She'd never lived in fear before and she wasn't about to start now. So she straightened her spine and tidied up the place, grateful that she had helpers as capable and Gavin and Koda to protect her.

Gavin had been on his laptop all morning and he'd had phone discussions back and forth with the crime lab and SAC Bridges. What had they learned?

She made some soup for lunch, washed her lab clothes and called the clinic again. Thankfully, they didn't have any holiday boarders, and no one had called with a sick animal, so she told the coworkers they could leave early.

"Lunch?" she asked Gavin now. Koda glanced up, hoping she might be offering him a meal.

Gavin grunted, then said, "I'll be right there."

He studied his laptop screen and then shut it with a slam. After they'd settled at the kitchen counter, hot vegetable soup and crackers in front of them, he said, "I've managed to follow Mack Creston's online footprint enough to gain a clear picture of the man. He's good at hiding things, but I'm good at finding things."

"Tell me," she said, dread making her appetite go away.

"I've traced him from Wyoming to Colorado. He joined the MSA five years ago."

"What?" Sydney shook her head. "He never told me he'd been a member that long, but he did go hunting and fishing a lot on the weekends. He'd leave for days and then call me wondering why I worked all the time. He hinted at moving in with me since I had more room. Of course, I didn't agree with that, which was the beginning of the end for us."

Gavin's gaze held appreciation and respect. "Well, he is a member of several outdoors clubs, but from what I can find, he's been kicked out of most of them for various reasons."

"Let me guess—drunk and disorderly, belligerent and a troublemaker?"

"You do know him well."

"I got to know him, yes. I was naive to believe anything the man said. I started dating him because of loneliness and he proved to be a great wilderness guide—showed me all the obvious places and some hidden places around here."

"I don't even want to think of you alone in the mountains with that man."

"Find him and bring him to justice."

Gavin nodded. "I promise I'll do that." Then he added, "Oh, Bridges called a few minutes ago. Samuels had a hidden safe under his bed at a secret safe house. He did manage to leave audio and video recordings there on a burner phone, and a flash drive with evidence that could bring down the whole organization."

Relief flooded through Sydney's system. "That's good. So when will that happen?"

"As soon as we can locate them. We need warrants and we'll have to substantiate the evidence. They tend to move around, but there is one main place where they hold what they call the High Meeting. That's where they plan their legitimate hunting-and-fishing tours, taking money from rich city folks to fund their other activities. Samuels never made it to any of the High Meetings, but his notes indicate they do a side hustle involving drugs and guns on the black market. A lot more profitable than being wilderness and mountain scouts for city fellows."

"Okay," she said, pushing away her soup. "But, Gavin, what has all of this got to do with me?"

Gavin took her hand. "I believe you were right. Mack is not happy that you're working for us, or maybe that you have a solid, legitimate career. He might have wanted you to join him and take care of their animals. They have horses, and cattle, too, on land they own, from what we can gather. You'd come in handy, but still be under his thumb."

"So when I broke it off, he set out to seek revenge."

"I think so. Especially after he found out about you moonlighting with RMKU."

She thought about that. "So we started dating a few months ago, and he talked about being a member of MSA, and proud of it. He did hint at taking me to a special camp, romantic and remote, but I wasn't ready for that."

"Thankfully," Gavin said. "Your instincts kicked in?"

"I think so, or maybe me being shy about dating," she admitted. "But, yes, after he showered me with gifts, I had to wonder what would be next. We hadn't gotten to know each other enough and I'd tried to avoid anything serious."

"Yeah, I know all about that," Gavin replied. "Some people aren't cut out for lifetime commitments."

"Right." She wondered if that was a hint to her. Not that she worried about Gavin. But he seemed to love family and traditions, even if he might not be ready for his own family yet.

"Anyway, he got more aggressive, and I became more distant and unsure. We had a horrible fight after he'd been away all week, but he tried to make up and then suggested he should move in with me. I ended it. I don't want that kind of chaos in my life, or in my relationships."

"Understood." Gavin got up to clear the counter. "It's odd you didn't hear from him before now."

"He's called once or twice, but he understood we wouldn't get back together. Now I'm wondering if he hasn't been watching me and waiting for the right time. If he's moved up the line with the MSA, then he could have the power to send people to do his dirty work."

"Yes, but one thing is missing from his profile, Doc. Most men like him want to do the dirty deeds themselves. It's personal, and he'd want to see you face-to-face. But he keeps sending others."

She followed Gavin's train of thought. "Are you thinking one day he'll be the one to show up and try to kill me?"

"Yes," Gavin said. "But, Sydney, he'll attempt to kidnap you first and take you into hiding, maybe to that special place he talked about."

Sydney shivered and wrapped her sweater tighter around her neck. "You're right. He'll want me to beg for my life, and he'll probably give me an ultimatum. Be his or no one will have me."

"Exactly," Gavin said, his expression grim.

Before they could finish that thread, her cell rang.

"Sydney, we've got trouble," Jennifer said. "Someone tried to break into the clinic, and Robert got injured trying to stop them. He's on his way to the ER."

Sydney glanced at Gavin. "I'll get there as soon as I can."

She ended the call and told Gavin what happened. "I need to get to the hospital."

Gavin immediately called Tyson to get someone to the clinic. Then he got Sydney and Koda into the SUV and headed for the hospital.

Sydney said a prayer and hoped Robert Whitson would be okay. She couldn't take another death.

Then her mind turned gritty. If Mack wanted to see her, she'd find a way to make that happen. And she'd end this somehow, one way or another.

FOURTEEN

The hospital was buzzing with activity as they entered the parking lot. Gavin had tried to reach the patrol they'd posted at the clinic. No answer and not much help sense the RMKU was scattered across the Rockies. He put away his phone and put on Koda's official vest, so he could bring the Malinois into the hospital.

"The doctors are in with him," the nurse informed Sydney when she rushed to the desk. "His wife is in the waiting room. Talk to her."

While Gavin made some calls, Sydney hurried around the corner and found Nan sitting with her hands held together, a full cup of coffee on the table next to her. The agony on her face broke Sydney's heart. "Nan?"

"Sydney," Nan said, rising to meet her. "I'm so glad you came."

"Of course," Sydney said. "Do you have any updates? The nurse said the ER doctors were still with Robert."

Nan nodded, her eyes misting over. "They hit him hard on the head. The doctors are trying to determine if he needs surgery or not. He's unconscious."

"I'm so sorry."

Nan looked confused and had tears in her eyes as she talked. "Jennifer said he took out the trash. She heard him talking loudly to another man. She ran to the back to see what was going on and found Robert lying on the ground with a bleeding head. But they didn't take anything. It's so hard to believe."

Sydney held Nan's hand in hers. "We will do whatever it takes to make sure he's okay. The doctors here are top-notch."

Nan nodded. "But why would anyone do this?"

Sydney glanced at Gavin again. "Someone is after me," she admitted. "I should have been there today."

"No, Robert said you'd taken some time off. This isn't your fault, Sydney. You could have been hurt or worse."

Sydney didn't deserve Nan's grace, but she accepted it even if she knew she'd left her employees in a bad way. "I should have gone to work, but we did have a patrol car watching the clinic."

Nan let out a gasp. "I didn't think about that. Robert couldn't tell me anything and Jennifer was so upset, I told her to go home."

Gavin held up a hand. "They also knocked out the police officer. He's here, too, but he's awake and talking."

Sydney's agitation turned to anger. "How did they manage that?"

They'd left the house so quickly, she hadn't thought beyond hearing about Robert being attacked. But it made sense they'd go after the officer guarding her clinic before they'd try anything.

"Gavin, is the officer going to be okay?" she asked.

"I'm about to find out," he said, walking toward the ER desk.

While he went to check on the officer, Sydney tried to console her friend. She'd known Robert and Nan since she'd moved here. Robert had helped her renovate the clinic, so she'd offered him a job. He loved animals as much as she did. His grandchildren often showed up to help clean the parking lot and help with some of the smaller animals. She often went to dinner at their house. They were more than friends. They were like a second set of parents to her.

She said a silent prayer for both of them, and for the officer who'd been hurt. She was losing hope that Mack and his criminal ring would be caught.

Why did he feel the need to harass her and try to kill her? What purpose could that serve, other than his vanity and insanity?

He wouldn't stop now, she knew. He was taunting her by hurting those close to her. How could she live with that guilt on her heart?

Gavin came back. "The officer is going to be okay. He was walking around out back when he got hit over the head. Has a mild concussion, but he's awake and anxious to get home to his wife. I'm going to take Koda and go to the clinic. If Koda can pick up a scent, we'll know which way they came from at least. If he picks up a scent he recognizes, we'll know it's the same person or people." He rubbed a hand over his hair and added, "We might get a break on fingerprints, too. These people are getting bolder, which means they'll make a mistake sooner or later."

"Yes, go," Sydney said, her mind on her employee.

He motioned to someone coming up the hallway. "I called Skylar Morgan to sit with you," he said. "Sydney, she goes where you go."

Sydney nodded, grateful to see another friendly face. Skylar was with the Denver PD and engaged to RMKU chief Tyson Wilkes.

"Hey, Gavin," Skylar said, her long red hair pulled back in a ponytail, her eyes scanning the ER waiting room. "Sydney, you hanging in there?"

Sydney didn't know Skylar very well since she was with a different team, but she'd been a liaison between the

Denver PD and the RMKU on a big case and everyone at
the unit knew what a dedicated cop she was.

She nodded. "Skylar, thank you. I'm okay. Just worried
about Robert and the officer who got hurt today."

Skylar eyed Gavin. "I've got this. Go do your thing."

Gavin gave Sydney one last look and left. She missed
him immediately then told herself not to do that. To take
her mind off things, after she introduced Skylar to Nan,
she asked, "How are things going with the wedding plans?"

"Good," Skylar said. "We're trying to keep things simple, but you know how that goes."

"Yes," Sydney said, wishing she could relax. "I'm sorry
you had to come and babysit me."

Skylar shook her head. "It's nice to get out for a bit. I
can only take so much advice from well-meaning friends
on how my wedding should go." Then she shook her head.
"And you don't need a babysitter. I heard how you took
down that first intruder with a needle full of sedatives."

Nan's eyes widened. "Sydney, you really are in danger.
You should come and stay with us."

"Thank you, Nan, but I think you'll be too busy taking
care of Robert. I'm being guarded, as you can see, and I
won't put you two in any more danger." She noticed Nan
kept glancing toward the ER doors. She hoped there would
be some good news very soon.

Sydney turned to Skylar. "I'm glad you're here. I want
these people to pay for what they've done. I hope you can
help find them."

Skylar leaned in. "I've been doing some research on the
side. The whole department wants in on this one. You're
important to the K-9 unit, Sydney. That means someone
is messing with someone we care about, and we don't like
that. Not at all. Gavin might be new here, but he's a dedicated officer. He'll find these people."

Sydney tried to speak but couldn't. She took a breath. "I wish I'd never dated Mack Creston."

Skylar squeezed her hand. "You're gonna make it through this, Sydney."

Nan sat across from them and nodded. "Sydney, you gave Robert a job he loved. We're blessed you came into our lives. These people won't get away with this."

Sydney prayed her friends were right, and she had to trust that God would see her through. And while she prayed, she hoped Gavin would stay safe out there trying to chase them down. He'd become an important person in her life.

A doctor came out of the ER wing and headed toward them, his expression hard to read. Now she prayed they'd hear good news. If something happened to Robert, she'd go after Mack Creston and let him know exactly how she felt about him. It could be the only way to get this weight off her shoulders, and to reclaim the life she loved.

And all the friends she cherished, too.

FIFTEEN

Tyson hurried up to Gavin. "Hey, man, we've got a solid print from the back door. I think the plan was to sneak in that way and do damage. But Robert Whitson scared the intruder at the clinic and when they scuffled, the guy must have grabbed on to the door facing. He left a print."

"That is good news," Gavin said, his gaze taking in the parking lot and the small rectangular building. "Sydney needs to hear something positive. This is beginning to get to her."

"Understandable," Tyson said. "I know how I felt all year long, being sabotaged and harassed. I hate seeing such a nice person going through the same."

Gavin nodded, remembering how someone had set out to seek revenge on Tyson for his brother's tragic death in the Middle East. "Let's hope we can stop this soon. Anything else?"

"Tire tracks from the field behind the clinic, so Koda was spot-on with his alert back there. Possible off-road vehicle. We've got the techs working on the boot design and we're still gathering information regarding who bought them and when. But that's a tedious search."

Gavin took in that information. "Koda picked up the scent and it led to the field. He lost the scent a few feet into the woods, though, so that would explain the ATV tracks."

"They probably came through a creek or spring," Tyson said. "But Koda put us on the right path. I've got people out searching in all directions and we've already picked up more tracks leading north."

"I can take Koda back out," Gavin said. "We'll start at the tracks you've found. He could pick up the scent again."

"I'll do it," Tyson said. "Echo's itching to work, and you need to get back to Sydney."

"Thanks," Gavin said. "I'm worried about her."

"We're getting closer, Gavin. Every little bit of evidence can bring us to the truth."

"It's a start. Let me know on the prints and the tracks. I'll keep working on the Terrain XX boot factor. If we can get an ID from the fingerprints, we can match that person to buying the boots. It's not much, but it can help."

Tyson made some notes, then glanced back at Gavin. "Hey, you okay?"

"Yeah, why do you ask?"

"You're taking this hard," Tyson said. "I know you like the doc and all, so I was wondering."

"Wondering what?" Gavin wasn't in the mood to make it easy for his friend.

"About your love life, or lack thereof," Tyson said with a sly grin. "Hey, I'm all for it."

"You would be since you're engaged," Gavin said. "Nothing to see here, however. I'm doing my job and trying to keep a friend and great veterinarian from being killed by a sociopath who used to be her boyfriend."

"Allegedly," Tyson cautioned. "We've still got to locate him and find something to pin on him."

Gavin's phone buzzed. "It's Bridges," he told Tyson. "Sir?" he said, answering the call.

"Gavin, we've found some significant news on Mack Creston," the SAC said. "Samuels left a lot of information hidden under that safe-house floorboard. We finally heard Mack Creston on video and found the notes Samuels left to back it up."

"So this means we have proof he's a member of MSA."

"Yes," Bridges said. "Samuels listed him as high priority and a real player. Willing to do whatever it takes to make it up the ranks."

Gavin let out a grunt. "Does that include him talking about trying to kill his ex-girlfriend?"

"Not yet, but Samuels did leave one cryptic comment in the margin of his notes."

"And what was that, sir?"

"'RMKU, question mark,' then a name—Sydney. Followed by the words 'MC will see her soon.'"

Gavin's pulse hammered like a hatchet hitting wood. "She told me Creston always said that to her and a man called her clinic after Samuels died and left that message."

"Okay, now we're getting somewhere," the SAC said. "Hey, once we're finished here, I might be out of commission over the next few weeks. A personal matter, so I'm hoping to go to my family's lake house for Christmas. I wanted to let the team know the latest."

"Roger, sir."

Gavin ended the call and filled in Tyson on the updates.

"Now we're cooking with gas," Tyson said. "Not much, but enough to get a fire under MSA, if we can find their current location."

"And if Mack Creston is running the show," Gavin added. Then he repeated Bridges' last words. "Got any idea what's eating at the SAC?"

Tyson shook his head. "No. He keeps things close to his vest, but whatever it is, I'm sure he has it under control."

"Right," Gavin said. "Now back to our regularly scheduled crime scene."

Tyson nodded and chuckled. "I'll keep you posted from my end while you get back to Doc Sydney. I hope things go well with her employee and our officer. No one should have a concussion during Christmas, especially one that came from some intruder trying to do harm."

"Thanks," Gavin replied, glad for Tyson's assistance.

"Oh, and by the way," Tyson said, "you're doing a great job. Don't forget that."

"I'll try not to," Gavin replied. "Once I know Sydney's safe."

Tyson's expression showed triumph. "You do have feelings for her, right?"

Gavin shrugged. "Can't say yet, but maybe."

And he left it at that.

In the ER waiting room, Sydney decided she wouldn't hide anymore. She'd only planned to take a few days off close to Christmas, but now her employees were in danger. She'd have to shut the clinic for a while.

She'd been distracted in so many ways, the main one being her attraction to Gavin. Work would give her focus, even if her employees took a break. She could still do paperwork, order supplies and clean the whole clinic. Always something to do.

She sat with Nan but made notes on her phone. Skylar paced and checked her phone, her shrewd gaze missing nothing.

Gavin walked in, Koda with him. Skylar shot him a glance then turned to give Sydney an eye-lift full of questions.

Sydney worked to control her relief and the sheer joy of seeing him alive and well. *Get it together.*

Gavin walked toward them, and Skylar fell into step beside him. "Any news?"

"A lot," he said, heading toward Sydney and Nan.

Sydney stood and met him in the space between the carefully lined up waiting-room chairs. "What?"

"First, how is Robert?" he asked.

Nan nodded to Sydney to speak. "He's still in a unconscious. We have to wait and see."

Sydney pushed at her hair and then held her hands together. "We're hopeful. It's only been a couple of hours, but we hope he'll wake up and show us he's okay."

Skylar's gazed moved back and forth between them. "So, Gavin, want me to hang out here or…are you back for the day?"

"And what did you find out?" Sydney added.

"Let's sit," he suggested.

Nan gave him a tired smile. "I'm going to the ER desk. I need to stretch my legs."

Gavin waited until Nan moved out of earshot and caught them up. "We have possible fingerprints, and we have concise video from Samuels, recording Mack Creston's voice. But the lab will run texts to confirm that. We also have Samuels's notes. He hid the real evidence well. We can now tie Mack Creston to the MSA, and we have a start in proving he's high up in the organization."

He gave Sydney a direct glance. "Samuels made a note about the RMKU and you, Sydney. Then he mentioned Mack saying he'd see you soon. Samuels made a point of that in his notes."

Sydney's hearted burned a warning with each beat. "He won't stop until he does see me," she said on a whisper.

SIXTEEN

Sydney felt sick—the coffee she'd had earlier was now roiling inside her stomach. "So Mack *is* the one behind this?"

"It looks like our suspicions were correct," Gavin said. "I'm sorry. We have to keep digging toward the evidence and bring him to justice. A man like that won't take no for an answer. The thrill of power does this with a lot of men."

"And especially one like what you described to me earlier," Skylar said.

Sydney had been honest with Skylar, hoping to get a detective's insight, and hoping for no more surprises.

Gavin checked both of them. "You two talked about this?"

"Yes," Sydney said. "Skylar's seen cases like this and she's doing her part to help."

"Agreed," he said. "I'm glad you had someone to talk to."

"I'm here to help," Skylar said. "What's next?"

Sydney said, "I plan to go back to my clinic and work. Just me," she added. "No employees or animals."

"What?" they both said.

"That's dangerous," Gavin told her, his eyes lighting fire.

"They won't dare come back there," she said. "I'll get a new alarm system and put up a fence if I need to."

"We don't have time for that. They're still out there," Gavin replied.

"I don't have time to sit around waiting," she countered.

"If you go, I go," he said. "You know Creston will show up sooner or later and you'd be unwise to try and confront him, Doc."

"I've been naive in dating him. I won't make that mistake again. Look, if I'm going about my business and we've got eyes on me, he could show up and you can zoom in and capture him. Meantime, as you said, we keep digging to find out where they're hiding out. It has to be nearby."

Skylar held a finger to her lips. "She does have a point. Make him think we're okay with this, that she's ignoring his threats. That'll get him riled up enough to come out into the open."

"And that's my first concern," Gavin said. "We all believe he'll be the one to get to you in the end—in his mind, anyway. You can't risk something going wrong, Sydney."

Skylar shifted on her black cowboy boots. "We can put a tap on the office phones and your phone, Doc. If he tries to reach out, we'll know." She glanced at Gavin. "He keeps sending people but none of them have managed to kill you. That could be because he wants you to be scared, thinking they'll kill you, but what he really wants is for them to bring you to him."

"And the whole Samuels mess?"

Gavin put his hands on her arms. "A setup. Samuels had to show loyalty, but he balked and panicked when it came to killing an innocent woman. Creston sent him in injured, so you'd be preoccupied that night. What better way for him to then just to walk in and take you?"

"Except you and Koda were there," she whispered, her heart bumping in a painful cadence. "Could he have been nearby?"

"I think he's been nearby with every attempt," Gavin

replied. "But you don't need to put yourself in danger to end this, which I know you want to do."

"I have to work," she said. "I'm going to work. You can either protect me there and at my home, or I'll protect myself."

"I'm in," Skylar said. "Gavin, we can take shifts."

Gavin studied Sydney's face then let out a sigh. "I'm still in. All in," he said. "I won't let him get near you."

Nan came back and had tears in her eyes. Sydney rushed to her, expecting the worst. "Nan?"

"He woke up," Nan said. "The nurse grabbed me and told me. I talked to him. He has a concussion, but the doctors are going to monitor him tonight and give us instructions when we get him home." Then she took Sydney's hand. "He doesn't remember much but he said to tell you the man who attacked him had the same tattoo as the man who came at you in the K-9 compound, Sydney."

Sydney gasped. "I did describe the tattoo to Robert to see if he would know anything about it. I'm amazed he remembered."

"MSA." Gavin's grim expression said it all. "We have to stay on you night and day, Doc. You understand that, right?"

She nodded, glancing at each one of them. "More than you'll ever know." Then she said, "But I intend to stay on course and do my job. I won't live in fear anymore."

Skylar patted Sydney's shoulder. "You're being smart, and we'll be smart about helping you."

Gavin tilted his chin. "More than you'll ever know," he said, mimicking her earlier words.

SEVENTEEN

They were about to leave for a quick bite when Gavin's phone buzzed. "Hey," he said to Sydney and Skylar, "the call is from a superstore I contacted earlier, regarding the Terrain XX boots."

"We'll be waiting in your SUV," Skylar said.

Gavin glanced around the nearly empty hospital parking lot, then unlocked the doors remotely.

Sydney and Skylar hurried ahead. Gavin gave Koda the go command. The dog followed and hopped into the open back of the SUV. Skylar watched the area until she had both Sydney and Koda safe.

"Mr. Flett," Gavin said, trying to sound positive, "were you able to find anything?"

Floyd Flett's gruff voice echoed through the phone. "It wasn't easy, Officer Walker, but between me and my right-hand person, Patsy Sanders, we hit on something that might help you with your case."

"Let me have it," Gavin said, his eyes constantly scanning the parking lot.

"About two months back, two men came in wearing dark clothes and looking for tactical gear. The video and the receipts we found show them buying boots, jackets and vests, along with some ammo and other supplies. Terrain XX boots are the most expensive style we carry. That's what stood out. Most aren't willing to pay this much, but hey, they are some of the best outdoor boots available. We happened to have five pairs on site. They each bought a pair for themselves and one for someone else."

"Can you send me copies of the video and the receipts?" Gavin asked, hope filling his heart. "This could be a big help."

"Sure, but it's hard to tell who they are by the video, and they paid in cold, hard cash."

"I'll check it out," Gavin said. "Thank you, Mr. Flett."

"Floyd," the man said. "You come by and see me if you need anything else."

Gavin ended the call and headed toward the SUV when a shot rang out. He ducked but felt the whiz of a bullet hitting his right shoulder. Grunting from the pain, he quickly got inside the vehicle.

"Get down. Now."

Then he cranked the SUV and sped away while Skylar covered them, her SIG Sauer peeking out the back passenger window. Another round of shots hit the air and sizzled against the bulletproof glass of the SUV.

"Coming from the left," Skylar said. "The west parking garage from what I can tell. I'm calling it in."

Gavin grunted again, his shoulder burning.

Sydney glanced over at him. "Gavin, you're hit."

He looked down at the blood seeping through his jacket. "I know. Just a scratch. It buzzed by me when I turned." He didn't tell her that if he'd been two seconds longer, the bullet would have come close to hitting her through the open driver-side door. "I'm okay. Are you?"

"No, I'm not okay," she said. "I want this over. Everyone around me is being threatened."

Gavin pulled the SUV into a side lot and listened as Skylar reported the shots fired. She turned to him. "Dispatch is sending some officers to cover it. I told them we were taking our subject to a safe place. They'll call us with an update."

"Call the guard at the hospital, too," Gavin said, gritting his teeth against the burn in his arm. "They should keep an eye on Mr. Whitson and his wife."

"I'm on it," Skylar said, her gaze holding his in the rearview mirror.

"Good," Gavin replied. "I'm taking the doc to the one place they can't get to her."

"Where is that?" Sydney asked.

"The RMKU headquarters," he said. "We'll be having an inside campout tonight."

And meanwhile, he'd go over everything Flett's Sporting World had sent him. They needed a break in this case before Sydney went rogue and tried to end this her way.

"This is about as safe as you can get," Gavin told Sydney later. "We've rounded up officers to guard the entire place." They'd settled into a conference room in the middle of the building. No windows, one door in and another one out. They had sleeping bags and Skylar had brought previsions—chips and sandwich stuff for now. And a cooler filled with water and drinks.

"This is ridiculous," she replied. "I appreciate it, but how long can I hide here, Gavin?"

"As long as it takes."

"I'll stay here tonight, but I want to get home soon. I've already called someone to install security at my house."

"I'll need to clear that," he replied.

"I did clear it," she responded forcefully. "I found a fully vetted security firm. Skylar's familiar with it and approved."

He nodded. "Tyson will keep us posted if they find anything, so hopefully that will be soon. The lab is going back over everything from Rick Samuels's clothes to the possible prints someone left at the clinic this morning."

Sydney fought against the stress and fatigue that pushed at her body. She'd doctored Gavin's arm, and he'd been right. Only a graze, but a nasty one. She'd cleaned it and put a topical antibiotic on it. Now she sat wondering what she could do to finally bring Mack Creston to justice.

"I've been racking my brain," she told Gavin after Skylar had gone to call Tyson. He and Skylar would provide extra protection along with Gavin keeping watch tonight. Tomorrow, one of them would escort her to work.

"About what?" Gavin asked, his eyes as weary as she felt.

"About Mack and any clues or hints I could use to help find him."

"Well, I'll ask some more questions and maybe you'll remember something. What does he like to eat?"

"Meat, grilled."

"What kind of music?"

"Country."

"Hobbies?"

"Hunting, fishing, being a nature scout."

"Family?"

She shook her head. "He lost his mother at a young age. His dad died of lung cancer a few years ago. He didn't talk about them much."

Gavin asked several more questions, but none brought up anything beyond basic tough-guy stuff.

"His favorite place in the mountains to hang out?" Gavin finally said before nibbling on a potato chip. "He's a hunter and fisherman, so he'd have some."

"He's been all over the state, of course. But he didn't tell me much about his travels." A glimmer of something floated through her head, but she couldn't put her finger on the memory.

Now that she thought about it, she and Mack hadn't talked much about personal stuff. She stayed busy, and he went on weekend scouting trips. No wonder their relationship hadn't lasted long. She could see now that he steered away from telling her anything personal. He didn't want to hear about her life, and he didn't want her to know too much about his.

Gavin set up his laptop so they could look at the store video from Mr. Flett. "You know, Flett's Sporting World isn't as big as some of the other outdoors stores. There's one on the east side of Denver and the main store near the Golden Gate Canyon State Park area. Does that ring a bell?"

Sydney stood and came to look at the video. "Yes," she said, the memory finally becoming clear in her head. "He told me once that his family had a piece of property not far from that park. He had a hunting permit there and he fished there, too." She sank back down. "That's about the only truly personal thing he ever told me—that he wanted to redo the old cabin and use it as a camp house, but when I questioned him more about it, he just laughed."

"Well, that's good information," Gavin said. "We can check it out."

Sydney's stomach roiled and her heart jittered and jumped. Would they finally be able to locate Mack and end this?

EIGHTEEN

The next day, she asked her neighbor to check on her animals, and then she went to work and immediately checked the office phone for messages.

Gavin came in with Koda and had the dog go through every room and closet. "All clear," he said to Sydney.

"Gavin, the office is still getting hang-up calls and a man asking for me," Sydney said. "I heard the messages and saw the number of dropped calls."

"Show me," Gavin said. Sydney took him to the phone and let the messages replay.

"That's Mack's voice," Sydney said. "He's good at hang-up calls and threatening messages."

"I'm going to forward this to the crime techs," Gavin said. "They might be able to pick up something in the background. I doubt there's a way to trace the calls. He's probably using a burner."

"He's too smart to leave a number, but I've seen him do this when he's mad at people. Harassment. He started on me after we broke up, but he finally stopped when I didn't respond. Now he's back. I am going to end this."

"I don't like the sound of that," Gavin said. "We need to let the techs go over it all, not plan a trap."

"You can help me," she retorted. "I'll meet him and talk to him, make him think I've had a change of heart—

or at least that I'm willing to listen to him. I'll explain he doesn't have to hurt others to get to me."

"No."

"You and Koda can be nearby. Your whole team can be nearby. I'll wear a wire and get him to admit everything. How else can this end? He knows how to disappear into the mountains."

"Yes, and he knows how to make you go with him."

"That can't happen if you're hiding close."

"I don't like this. We can't predict these things, and something could go wrong."

"Think about it while I call Nan to see how Robert's doing."

After hearing a good report, she told Nan to make sure he took as long as he needed. Nan assured her the prayers and good wishes of so many were helping. Then she turned to find Gavin standing there, his gaze full of worry and something else.

A longing.

The same longing she could feel in her heart.

But, no, she couldn't fall for a man this quickly, and certainly not after what she'd been through. Yet each time he looked at her or touched her, she felt a thrill that she'd never felt with the few men she'd dated. Mack hadn't made her feel this way, so why had she even bothered with him?

You didn't feel worthy.

That realization hit her like a ton of bricks. She'd had such a low self-esteem due to her upbringing, she'd settled for any man who'd give her a second glance and that had been the wrong way to go about it.

Gavin made her feel worthy, made her feel safe, made her happy. Even with her life threatened, she felt something in her heart that glowed with a warmth that gave her peace.

"What are you thinking?" he said as he walked closer.

"That I'm truly blessed in knowing you," she admitted.

He reached a hand to her cheek. "Sydney..."

"Not yet," she said, taking his hand in hers. "But once this is over."

"Yes, when this is over." He stepped back. "I don't like your plan."

"Got anything better?"

"Not yet. But I'm trying to piece it all together. Will you give me time to do that—at least a couple more days?"

"I want this over."

"So do I," he said, his blue eyes moving over her face. "Now more than ever."

While Koda followed Sydney around during her cleaning routine, Gavin went back over the copies of the receipts Mr. Flett had sent him. All cash, so nothing to trace there. But the dates stood out. About a week before the attacks on Sydney.

He called the tech lab to see if they'd found anything.

"Gavin, glad you called," the head technician said. "We made a print from the boots Mr. Samuels had on the night he entered the RMKU compound."

Gavin's pulse quickened. "And?"

"And they match the prints found at the Jones Clinic, only the person at the clinic wears a smaller size."

"Okay, give me the two sizes."

"One is a twelve and the other is a ten wide."

"The smaller one is from the clinic yard?"

"Yes. And the boots are definitely the same as the ones Mr. Flett sent to compare. They had to have come from that store."

"What about hair fibers and fingerprints?"

"We found some fibers on Samuels's jacket. Mostly his, but we're still running a few darker ones. About to work on the fingerprints. Believe me, we've covered Samuels's clothing and any hair or fluid samples."

"Okay, thanks." Gavin ended the call, hope resurfacing.

He turned and walked down the hallway, thinking of how gentle Sydney was with the animals. Although she'd cleared the place out due to the circumstances, he found her sitting in an exam room with Koda standing guard nearby.

"Hey, you okay?" he asked, as he leaned a shoulder on the doorjamb.

She looked up, her expression full of hurt and loss. "I thought so, but this is hard. Empty exam rooms, no boarders—it's so quiet here. Too quiet. I wanted to work, but that's all been halted, hasn't it? People can't bring their animals to a place that might be dangerous." Lowering her head, she said, "He's doing it, Gavin. He's ruining my life."

Gavin lifted her up. "We're gonna fix that, Doc."

"Yes. He wants me, so he can think he's worn me down. When I see him face-to-face—"

"That's why you can't," Gavin said. "That right there. You'll be so full of anger when you confront him and that's a dangerous thing."

"It's our last resort, Gavin. Rick Samuels tried to bring him in and look what happened to him."

"I'm working on every angle."

Her tone changed. "I know you are, and I am so glad you're here with me. I don't want anything else to happen. I—I couldn't take losing you, too."

Gavin gave up on protocol and pulled her to him. "You will not lose me, even when this is over."

"If it's ever over."

He tugged her closer, so close he could see brown flecks in her dark eyes. "You have to know how I feel."

Sydney blinked, lifted her head. "I do. And that's why I want this over."

He kissed her, to prove he wanted to be here with her.

She returned the kiss with a sigh.

Koda let out a low woof.

They broke apart. "Not yet," she said. "After I know we're both safe. If Mack has any inkling that we've grown close, he'll make you the next target."

NINETEEN

SAC Bridges called Gavin as they were headed to Sydney's house to check the animals.

"I have news. Can you come to my office?"

"We're on our way," Gavin said, turning the SUV around.

Sydney's dark expression changed. "A break in the case?"

"Maybe, since he asked to see me in person," Gavin said. "Can you call Roscoe to take care of the animals? This might take a while."

She made the call. "He's on his way over. He has a key to my house, and he said patrol cars have checked every thirty minutes today."

"Right on schedule," Gavin said. "And you'll have coverage tonight, too." He watched the road and continued, going over everything out loud. "We know the boots came from Flett's Sporting Goods near Golden Gate Canyon State Park. We have the time stamp of the day they were bought, and we've sent the grainy images to the lab to see if they can enlarge them for facial recognition. We even have the boot sizes. One fit Rick Samuels. The other is a smaller foot."

"What size?" she asked, her hand holding onto the door handle.

"Ten wide. Ring a bell?"

Sydney nodded. "Mack's size. He always took his boots off when he came to visit. I cleaned them up once or twice and noticed the size."

"Okay, that's good," Gavin said. "Something to add to the evidence." He headed back up the county road toward the interstate. "We should get reports on any fibers found on Rick Samuels's body, and any prints found at my place, your place and the clinic." He heaved a sigh. "The only thing we haven't checked is the cabin you mentioned. I did pull up a map, but any structures are few and far between, and since we don't know the exact location, that could take a while."

They were almost to the interstate when Sydney's phone rang. "It's my neighbor, Roscoe," she said.

Gavin waited as she listened. Then she said, "We'll be there soon."

She ended the call. "Gavin, I have to get home. Roscoe says Herman is missing. The back fence has been cut open."

"Someone took your horse?" Gavin went onto the interstate and crossed to get to the nearest turnaround. "Let me call this in, so Bridges won't wonder what happened."

He made the call and then started back toward her house. "Just one more trick up Creston's sleeve."

Sydney ran toward the barn but didn't see her neighbor. "Roscoe?"

When she saw the empty stall, she ran to the back and saw the gaping fence. Turning toward the house, she called to Gavin. "I don't see Roscoe. I thought he called from here."

"And I don't see the cruiser," Gavin called from where he was standing at the SUV. "Wait, Sydney."

Gavin called for backup, but when Sydney heard

Repeat squawking, she kept running. She hurried into the house. "Roscoe?"

"He's unavailable right now."

She stopped and gulped a breath when she saw Mack standing there with a gun aimed at her. "What did you do to Roscoe?"

"Roscoe," Repeat said. "Roscoe."

"Tell that bird to shut up," Mack said, his voice like cold steel.

"Shut up, shut up," Repeat said.

"He's scared," Sydney replied, gathering her strength, her eyes scanning the room for a weapon.

"Don't even try, sweetheart," Mack said, outguessing her. "You think I don't know your every mood or move? I've been tracking you since you broke things off with me."

He went to her tote bag and pulled out a circular key-like object. "Easy-peasy to tuck a tracker into the lining of that big tote bag you carry around."

That explained too many things she didn't want to think about right now. She stayed silent when he dropped it into his vest pocket. She still had her phone hidden in the deep pocket of her heavy twill work pants. She prayed someone would be able to track them.

"Okay, then since you know all about me, let's talk," she suggested. "Is Roscoe okay?"

Mack's chuckle crackled down her backbone. "Oh, now you want to talk." He was wearing camouflage and the same boots she and Gavin had discussed. He'd grown a beard and his hair bushed out in a messy crown. "Don't worry, your devoted neighbor is okay. Just tied up in a safe place."

Sydney tried to calm down. Gavin would be here soon with Koda. "What do you want, Mack?"

"You," he replied. "I couldn't seem to get you out of my mind, but I got busy with work. But then I tracked you to

the Rocky Mountain K-9 Unit, where you've been working extra hours. Sydney, you should have warned me."

"About what? Where I work is none of your business."

"You will always be my business," he retorted. "I held
back on getting in touch for personal reasons, but my status has changed over these last few months. Now we can
finally catch up without being interrupted. You'll get to
see my cabin."

"Your cabin near the park," Sydney said, her mind burning with rage as she hoped Gavin and Koda would be here
soon. "The cabin you always talked about?"

Mack nodded his head. "Our secret hideaway. I got it
ready for you. Herman is waiting—better to take a horse—
and we're going for a ride."

"No, you're not," a voice said from behind him.

Gavin! He'd come through the back door. Sydney let out
a sigh of relief, her body shivering with fear and adrenaline. Koda snarled a growl.

Mack glanced over his shoulder. "I think you're wrong,
Officer Walker. I have a gun on Sydney and if you or that
dog make one move, I'll shoot her and then I'll kill both
of you."

Repeat squawked and flapped his wings. "Gun! Gun!"

"Mack," Sydney said, shaking her head at Gavin, "I'll
go with you. I want to talk to you because I don't want
anyone else to get hurt because of me."

Mack advanced and grabbed her by the arm.

Behind him, Gavin stepped closer.

"Don't come any farther," Mack said, pivoting to hold
Sydney in front of him like a shield. "She's mine. She'll
always be mine and she can't work for you people. She'll
work for me. I've got big plans and I need a supportive
wife by my side."

Gavin inched a little closer, Koda right beside him.

"You are not taking her," he said, the words dropping like rocks into the air, his eyes on Sydney.

"Yes, I am." Mack held the gun on Gavin and Koda. "You'll never have her."

"No!" Sydney screamed, lifted her arm and pushed as Mack fired two rounds. Then he pushed her out the door she'd left open in her haste.

Gavin fired back, hitting Mack's left arm. Koda barked and growled then leaped into the air.

But Mack slammed the door shut just as Koda reached them.

Pulling her down the steps, Mack said, "If you fight me, Sydney, the dog will be next." He pointed his gun toward the closed door.

"No," Sydney said. "No, Mack." Taking one last look back, she nodded. "I'll go with you."

She could hear Koda's aggressive barks and the sirens in the background, but it was too late. She'd never make it out of this alive now. And she'd never be able to tell Gavin she had fallen for him.

TWENTY

Gavin groaned and stood, his already injured arm burning with yet another shot. "Koda, come!"

The dog dropped from scratching at the door and hurried toward Gavin.

Gavin held his arms out as officers rushed in. "I'm okay," he explained. "Check Koda."

Michael Bridges held back Gavin as he headed toward the door. "We got here as soon as we could. I wanted you to know Creston's been tracking Sydney."

Gavin stopped, then turned around. Someone handed him a bottle of water. He drank it down then stared at the SAC. "Tracking? We checked her place and her car."

"On her person," Bridges explained. "He used a key-finder electronic tracker—you know, the newfangled kind. We were finally able to get a handle on his online footprint. Found an email receipt showing he'd ordered the gadget a while back."

Gavin regained his senses quickly after that revelation. "Where are they now? Did you take him into custody?"

Tyson came in, shaking his head, Echo on his heels. Then he looked at Gavin. "I'm sorry, man. He took Sydney."

Gavin threw his empty water bottle across the room. "I—I blew it. I have to find her."

"Whoa, cowboy, you need to be checked over," Bridges

said. "We spotted them on horseback but couldn't get in a clean shot. We have people on the trail."

Gavin headed to the door. "I'm taking Koda, and we'll find her."

He glanced around. Koda was standing alert and ready. Sydney would be smart about this. She'd try to stay alive because she was tough. And because they had unfinished business between them.

He loved her. More than he'd realized, probably from the first time he'd met her.

"Gavin, we can't go off without all the info," Tyson told him. "Take a minute. Regroup. We've got evidence, we know it was him, all of it, from the boots he wore, the tricks he played sending others to distract us, and he had an FBI undercover informant murdered. The man will get his time, I promise."

"But he has *her*, Tyson," Gavin said. "Mack Creston has Sydney, and he won't give her up without a fight."

"Mack," Repeat said, squawking. "Mack! Fight!" Then the bird twisted his head. "Cabin. Cabin. Cabin."

Gavin stood. "A cabin. Sydney remembered a cabin near the Golden Gate Canyon State Park. That has to be where he's been hiding out."

"Cabin," Repeat said, squawking. "Cabin. Cabin."

Gavin nodded. "Even the bird knows that." Then he went to her tote bag and searched through it. "He must have taken the tracking device with him, which means if Sydney has her phone, I should be able to pick up a signal." He gave them all one last glance. "And I'm going to find her."

Sydney watched as Mack slapped Herman to send the roan back to her place. He winced, blood trailing down from the hole in his canvas jacket. Then he forced her into a truck, and they were now headed along a dark dirt trail through the foothills, making it impossible for her to get her bearings. But Mack hadn't checked the inside pocket of her heavy jacket, where she'd stored her phone.

Now she prayed Gavin would figure out she had her phone, and somehow pick up the tracking signal. It was the only way he'd ever find her.

"We'll be all right now," Mack said. "You'll be the official vet for the MSA. We'll rule together, you and me, just as I've planned."

Her heart thudded so loudly she felt sure he could hear it. She wouldn't help with his wound. She prayed he'd pass out, or that she could find a way to wound him even more. "I'd like to hear more about this plan," she said. "I have my clinic to consider."

"I'll build you a new clinic and we'll have our own animals. You'll love it, Sydney."

Sydney's prayers kept her focused. She could do this. She'd find a way to escape. But she wasn't sure where she'd wind up in this vast terrain. "Tell me about the cabin," she finally said.

"You'll really love it," Mack retorted with a laugh. "I've got a high fence around the property. No one can get in or out. You'll be safe there until we can move to the big mountain retreat in the high country."

The High Rockies meant high up in remote areas of the mountains. Even more remote than what sounded like a prison he'd built near the park. He'd never let her go. She'd be trapped and she'd have to do his bidding or die.

Sydney stayed quiet. She'd wait until they got to the cabin, then she'd find a way to knock him out and take his truck. He'd lost a lot of blood but chose to ignore that. She wouldn't treat his wound. And she'd break down any walls he'd built to hold her in.

Gavin knew the direction they'd gone. Herman had come back with drops of blood on his saddle, and they'd found Roscoe tied up in his own house. Now Gavin slowly drove through a rough trail, where Koda had alerted. But it was tedious work. He kept eyeing his phone, using the little moving spot on the map as his guide. He'd drive a while then stop and look for tire tracks, Koda's air sniffs showing him the way, the tracker keeping pace. He'd lose the signal if he didn't hurry.

Tyson put a backup team together to follow, so they could surround the property.

But where was the property?

He stopped and pulled up his phone map again, hoping he wouldn't lose service. The trails closely followed 93 North to the park entrance, but the tracking device wasn't so good in the deep woods. The cabin had to be near there.

Golden Gate Canyon State Park was about an hour west of Sydney's place and there were trails and back ways all in between. They'd quickly studied the map and tried to match trails, but in the dark, this was a maze.

He'd have to trust his judgment, and Koda's spot-on accuracy, but he'd have to trust in God. Because prayer was the main thing leading him right now.

He followed the trails leading northwest. The snow grew heavier here, so between the moonlight and his SUV lights, he spotted fresh tire tracks. Creston had slowly made his way between the foothills and moved across a valley. Gavin reported in and kept going. He didn't have any choice once the electronic tracker stopped working.

Now he stood in the thicket of woods and rocks, alone with his faithful partner. "It's just you, me and the Lord," he told Koda when they stopped to check the tracks.

Gavin took a moment to look up into the sky and caught a glimpse of the evening star. That would be his guide.

"I'm coming, Doc. I promise."

Then he got back in the SUV and drove as fast as possible to catch up with Mack Creston and Sydney.

* * *

"We're here, darling. You're gonna love this place."

Sydney doubted that. The way he'd been ranting about this cabin, she'd be his prisoner and she'd be expected to do his bidding, no questions, no arguments.

She focused on her prayers and on how much she cared for Gavin. The contrast between Mack and Gavin was remarkable. She'd fought her feelings for Gavin because she'd had too many bad relationships. But now, she understood she was worthy of a man who could match her in strength, integrity and honor. Not only match her own values, but also go above and beyond for the people he cared about. She wanted to be one of those people.

Mack used a remote to open the massive gate, then drove the truck inside. The gate automatically closed behind him. He might be living off the grid, but he had electricity.

Once they were inside, she took in her surroundings, the faint glow of a security light casting out shadows deep into the trees and outbuildings. Then she spotted the true cabin, which looked more like a squatty rectangular box with shuttered windows and a heavy wooden door. Her prison.

Mack's sinister smile and deep chuckle only added to her fears. "Welcome home, darling."

Sydney had run out of options. Mack had quickly turned mean once he had her inside the cabin. "You'll live in here for a while," he said in a conversational tone that felt like spiders tickling her spine. "Until you know to do better, understand?"

Before she could protest, he tossed her into a dark square room with a door that was made of steel bars—a big cage. Mack stood inside the opening, one hand against the bars, smiling at her. "Comfy, isn't it?"

Her nerves tangled into a mass of rage and fear as she

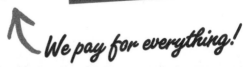

YOU pick your books –
WE pay for everything.
You get up to FOUR New Books and TWO Mystery Gifts...absolutely FREE!

Dear Reader,

I am writing to announce the launch of a huge **FREE BOOK GIVEAWAY**... and to let you know that YOU are entitled to choose up to FOUR fantastic books that WE pay for.

Try **Love Inspired® Romance Larger-Print** books and fall in love with inspirational romances that take you on an uplifting journey of faith, forgiveness and hope.

Try **Love Inspired® Suspense Larger-Print** books where courage and optimism unite in stories of faith and love in the face of danger.

Or TRY BOTH!

In return, we ask just one favor: Would you please participate in our brief Reader Survey? We'd love to hear from you.

This FREE BOOKS GIVEAWAY means that your introductory shipment is completely free, <u>even the shipping</u>! If you decide to continue, you can look forward to curated monthly shipments of brand-new books from your selected series, always at a discount off the cover price! <u>Plus you can cancel any time</u>. Who could pass up a deal like that?

Sincerely

Pam Powers

Pam Powers
For Harlequin Reader Service

Complete the survey below and return it today to receive up to 4 FREE BOOKS and FREE GIFTS guaranteed!

FREE BOOKS GIVEAWAY
Reader Survey

1

Do you prefer books which reflect Christian values?

◯ YES ◯ NO

2

Do you share your favorite books with friends?

◯ YES ◯ NO

3

Do you often choose to read instead of watching TV?

◯ YES ◯ NO

YES! Please send me my Free Rewards, consisting of **2 Free Books from each series I select** and **Free Mystery Gifts**. I understand that I am under no obligation to buy anything, no purchase necessary see terms and conditions for details.

❑ **Love Inspired® Romance Larger-Print** (122/322 IDL GRQV)
❑ **Love Inspired® Suspense Larger-Print** (107/307 IDL GRQV)
❑ **Try Both** (122/322 & 107/307 IDL GRQ7)

FIRST NAME	LAST NAME

ADDRESS

APT.#	CITY

STATE/PROV.	ZIP/POSTAL CODE

EMAIL ❑ Please check this box if you would like to receive newsletters and promotional emails from Harlequin Enterprises ULC and its affiliates. You can unsubscribe anytime.

LI/LIS-122-FBG22_LI/LIS-122-FBGVR

took in the small cot and one straight-back chair. She grabbed the cord of her hoodie and twirled it, not knowing what to do. And then an idea popped into her head as she glanced down at the heavy cord in her hand. "You'll regret this, Mack. Someone will find me."

"How?" he shouted. "There isn't a cell tower anywhere around here."

He turned to go at the same moment she managed to tug the silky cord out of the hood. It came loose, was free in her hands. This was her last opportunity, so she lunged at his back and looped the cord over his head and around his neck, then she twisted the string as tight as she could. She only wanted him to pass out so she could run.

Mack struggled, his previous wound gushing blood, his hands flailing in the air as he pushed forward, trying to fight her. But Sydney held tight, kicking at him. Now past the cell door, he fell back toward the bars, hitting his wound, and causing the door to slam shut, with him outside and her inside. Sydney held tight as she was propelled forward. She was a prisoner now. She let go of the strings, but Mack struggled to get free of the cord still tightly caught against his neck. He glanced back at her, fear in his eyes as he struggled and twisted but the cord stretched tautly, cutting into his skin, the two ends caught between the shut door and the bars behind him. Then he slid down and settled his head again the cold metal.

Sydney screamed, from fear and rage and relief.

He'd die. And no one would ever find her in this locked room. Because she couldn't reach the key.

TWENTY-ONE

Gavin lost the trail. He left the SUV and put Koda's snow socks on so they could walk the rest of the way.

Koda sniffed the ground and air, lifting his nose high. Stopping, he turned to Gavin.

"Which way, boy?"

Koda turned back toward some dense woods.

"It'd have to be the hard way, right."

Creston must have turned back onto a road somewhere in these woods. They'd need to find that road.

Thirty minutes later, Gavin let out a sigh of relief as they hit an old logging trail with a pockmarked, partially paved lane. Then he saw the faint shadow of glowing lights through the woods.

"It's showtime," he whispered. He managed to get a message to Tyson, sending him the location that had pinged on his electronic map. With GPS, Tyson could be here in under an hour.

But Gavin didn't plan on waiting. "Let's go, Koda. We've got work to do."

They moved through the snowy woods, creating very little sound, and made it to the high wooden wall around the place.

Gavin studied the gate, figuring it had sensors. He'd have to find a back way in. That didn't take long since the cabin backed up the mountainside. Using a penlight, he discovered a trapdoor probably built as an escape hatch, and after some careful maneuvering, managed to pry it open with a stout limb. After a drop down onto a dirt floor, he and Koda were inside the house.

He tiptoed his way up the cellar stairs when he heard a scream. Then he heard what sounded like a heavy thump. "Help me!"

"Go," he shouted to Koda. They both ran up the rickety stairs, Koda barking and snarling. With one booted foot, Gavin knocked open the old door and ran into the muted darkness of a short hallway. Around a corner, his gun out, he found a kitchen lit with low lights.

"Sydney?"

"I'm here," she called from what looked like a caged door. Smothering a sob, she said, "Gavin, you came."

He took in the scene as Koda rushed to where Creston was lying against the bars of the door, a dark cord tight against his neck. "What happened?" Gavin asked, checking the man's pulse. "Weak, but alive." Creston had blood all over his shirt.

"He...forced me inside," she said. "It didn't go very well."

Gavin found a key on Creston's belt. "Which one?"

"The big one," she said, her hand shaking.

Gavin got the heavy barred door open and pulled her into his arms. "You've alive. You're okay."

She nodded against his jacket and held tight. "Yes, and I'm never letting go of you."

Gavin held her tight. "Same," he whispered.

Then he figured out what she'd done.

"You used the cord from your hoodie as a weapon?"

"Yes." She pulled back. "I managed to keep pulling on it until I had it hidden in my hand. When he turned to lock me in, I lifted it and threw it around his neck, pulling hard.

Then I jabbed him against the bars, making sure his wound got hit. We struggled and…he pushed against the door and got out from the cage. But his weight caused the door to slam shut with the cord caught between it and the bar."

"Trapping him."

She nodded. "I let go, but he passed out. I was trying to find a way to reach for the key when I heard you and Koda."

Gavin nodded, kissed her head and sat her down on an old chair. "Why don't we lock him inside that cage while we wait for backup? I think he'll live."

"Great idea," she said. "But before anyone gets here, there's one thing."

"Yeah, what's that?"

She grabbed Gavin and kissed him, her hands on his neck. Then she pulled back. "You did say when this was over, right?"

"We both said, that, yes." Gavin kissed her again, and thanked God he'd found this woman.

EPILOGUE

Gavin woke with a start, then remembered they were all safe. Sydney was back at her house and Mack Creston was under lock and key at an undisclosed hospital. He should go to prison based on all the evidence they'd gathered. The RMKU and the Denver PD launched a major investigation on the MSA group after finding drugs and guns inside Mack's cabin.

Of course, Gavin had slept in his truck outside of Sydney's house, just because she'd been so exhausted and traumatized.

"C'mon, Koda," he said as he let out the K-9 and headed toward the porch to knock. The sun shimmered a bright smile to the east. He needed coffee.

He heard footsteps coming up the hallway inside, then he saw her there in a long robe and her flannel pajamas. "You look right at home."

She motioned him inside and made coffee. After pouring him a cup, she settled on the couch beside him and asked, "Are you sure about this?"

"About you and me, uh, yes."

"Okay."

He put down his coffee, dragged her close and kissed her. "Why do you ask?"

"I said I'd never wanted to…have a relationship again."

He laughed. "I think we both said that."

"But you, Gavin, you are the best man I've ever known."

Gavin touched a hand to her cheek. "We are going to have a great Christmas, Doc. Meantime, we've got plenty of time to finally go on a date."

She jumped up and went to the Christmas tree. "I ordered this and had it delivered to the clinic. Then I had Roscoe put it under the tree."

"For me?"

She nodded. "Open it. We need a celebration."

Gavin opened the big box and pulled back the paper.

"A *milagro* tree?"

"I wanted us to have one. Like your mother said, tiny miracles happen every day. We just need to find them."

Gavin lifted the tree-shaped flat metal piece of art out of the box and stood it on the table.

She dug something else out. "Our first ornament."

"Really," he said, holding up the silvery little treasure made in the shape of a sitting dog. "Koda, of course."

She smiled. "Of course." Koda woofed his approval.

"I love you," Gavin whispered, his voice husky with emotion.

"I love you, too."

They'd forgotten to cover Repeat's cage. "Love," the bird repeated. "Love you. Love you."

Gavin laughed and pulled Sydney back into his arms, the Christmas charms from the little metal tree winking up at him in agreement. God had brought him home, at last.

* * * * *

Dear Reader,

I hope you enjoyed Gavin and Sydney's Christmas story. I loved Koda, the K-9 hero of this story.

I always love writing stories about friends who fall in love. Gavin didn't think he was ready to settle down after dealing with a tragedy during a military mission, and Sydney didn't want a rebound romance after the trauma of breaking up with her boyfriend.

God had other ideas for these two. He brought them together under the worst of circumstances. Christmas has a way of finding the good, even when you're chasing bad guys. Gavin had a lot to prove to the team, and Sydney had a lot to prove to herself. They both found their courage and strength in getting this case done and over.

God sometimes puts us in places where we are not comfortable, but He gives us the courage and strength to make the right decisions at the right time. I hope wherever you are in your faith journey, you'll remember Gavin and Sydney and their little Christmas tree, and Koda there watching over them.

And I hope you will know that you are not alone, and you do have the courage and strength to get through the worst, with God's love behind you all the way.

Until next time, may the angels watch over you. Always.

Lenora Worth

SILENT NIGHT EXPLOSION

Katy Lee

To Jason,

Keep looking up. Your help comes from the Lord.

While we look not at the things which are seen,
but at the things which are not seen:
for the things which are seen are temporal;
but the things which are not seen are eternal.
—*2 Corinthians* 4:18

ONE

Light traveled faster than sound, so when Rocky Mountain K-9 Unit admin Jodie Chen saw the flames skyrocket up from somewhere in downtown Denver, she knew an explosion would quickly follow. She raced to her black Labrador in the backyard training facility at the RMKU and held her breath as a loud blast knocked her to her knees.

She covered Shiloh with her upper body and burrowed her fingers and face deep into his thick black coat. The Labrador trembled beneath her at the shock, but he quickly pushed himself up to stand, taking a guard position to protect her, just as she had for him. It was times like these that she wondered why Shiloh failed the assessment to be a K-9 officer at the RMKU. And it was also times like these that she knew he had it in him to be an amazing protector. When everyone else had crossed him off the list, she chose to continue to work with him on her own time—early in the morning, before the handlers arrived.

Another explosion blasted through the air, and Jodie signed the command to "stay" as she reached for her cell phone in her back pocket. Her mother was Deaf and signed with American Sign Language, so Jodie tended to use sign-language cues as well as verbal ones with the dogs. She felt Shiloh's timidity warranted a gentler approach, which signing could offer. And with the explosions going on around them, she was glad she didn't have to yell over them for Shiloh to understand. She had hoped he could be used in cases with people who were Deaf, and she had her first call from a potential match that morning. Unfortunately, the woman had been a no-show.

Monica Malone had contacted Jodie through a video-conference system for the Deaf. She'd said that it was urgent for her to get protection from someone from her work who meant her harm. She hadn't wanted to give too many details over the video call, but Jodie surmised Monica knew something that put her in danger. Jodie looked at the billowing smoke over the east side of Denver and thought perhaps Monica wasn't a no-show at all. Jodie wondered if there could be a correlation.

Her phone buzzed in her hand. A spark of hope of it being Monica was dashed away when the caller ID said *Victor Abrams*.

Victor was RMKU's newest handler, hired about three weeks ago. Ordinarily, she welcomed the new recruits in, but she recently uncovered something from his past that made her question if he should be protecting anyone. She had already been working as the administrative assistant for Sergeant Tyson Wilkes, the head of RMKU, for nearly a year, since the unit began. Her job was to pull the background checks on criminals as well as employees, but Victor's security check had come back squeaky clean—then she found a newspaper article that raised a red flag.

If she didn't tell her boss what she'd uncovered soon, Tyson would start giving Victor his own cases. His probationary period was about to end, and that meant the team would trust him to have their backs. She looked at the screen and wondered about the man's innocence. More than anything, she wanted him to be innocent, but she had to ask herself if that was because she found him extremely attractive. He had light brown hair with flecks of gold and piercing blue eyes that captured her attention the moment he'd arrived at the unit, and a strong, muscular body that his twelve years as a US Navy SEAL had formed.

Guilt over letting a handsome man blind her to her duties made Jodie send his call to voice mail.

Then her phone buzzed again. Jodie sighed, knowing the caller ID would read *Victor Abrams* again before she even looked at it.

But it didn't. It read *unknown caller.*

She sat up as sirens could be heard off in the distance rushing to the explosion. It was a video call, and she knew it had to be Monica. Jodie clicked to join but was only met with a dark screen. She could see the person on the other end was shuffling or running. Calling out to her would make no difference when Monica couldn't hear. Jodie peered at the screen and realized she was looking at smoke. She lifted her eyes above the phone to take in the billowing flames on the outskirts of Denver.

Monica was in that fire.

Jodie shouted to the phone, "I'm on my way! Stay with me." She signed the words, hoping that Monica would be able to see her. "Shiloh, come!" Jodie gave the sign as she ran toward the back entrance of the RMKU headquarters. After a few steps she realized Shiloh hadn't moved.

Looking back at the dog's hesitancy, Jodie could see this was why he had failed the assessment. He needed coaxing, and in an emergency, time was critical. Taking him now could be destructive, but he understood sign language.

Jodie raced back to him and grabbed him by his black vest collar. The words *Rocky Mountain K-9 Unit* were printed on the sides. The only thing different between his vest and those of the other handlers' dogs was that Shiloh never earned his badge. The RMKU handlers might say he was a glorified pet.

But Jodie just couldn't give up on him. Not yet. She

also knew the handlers would say she'd grown too attached to the dogs.

Leading Shiloh to the back entrance, Jodie pushed up
her tortoiseshell glasses over her nose so she could read
the access pad. She punched in the code and the door unlocked. Racing inside, she passed the conference room
and the bullpen with the handlers' cubicles. Not a person
was in sight. Even Tyson's office had been locked up for
the Christmas holiday. She came to a skid across the shiny
wood floors by the office Christmas tree, with its cute dog
ornaments. She tried to think of her next steps.

Then she heard a sound from the bullpen. A chair
creaked, and a head popped up from behind a cubicle
partition.

Victor Abrams was the only handler around.

He pulled a set of earphones from his ears. "I just called
you," he said. "I thought we could grab lunch. I mean, if
you want to." He shrugged, and she knew he sensed her
concern about him. He'd been trying hard to win her over.
He had even brought her daisies last week. She didn't tell
him it was her favorite flower.

"I need to contact Tyson," she said urgently. "An explosion just happened on the east side. A civilian who called
the unit for protection is in it."

Jodie glanced at her office, which was adjacent to
Tyson's closed door. Four large monitors were lit up with
various tasks and background checks that she had been
running earlier, including Victor's. She may have been
training Shiloh out back, but that wasn't her job. Her job
was sitting at that desk and getting information for the handlers in their cases…and making sure the handlers could
be trusted with cases.

But Monica needed her.

Jodie looked back at her phone and watched as the connection was lost.

"No!" She tried to redial. It went nowhere. She had no time to call Tyson.

Jodie had no choice. "Victor, I need your help."

The news of a bomb detonating on the outskirts of Denver near his new place of employment nearly had Victor Abrams frozen in place. Every instinct in him told him this move had been a bad idea. His military career in explosives had ended traumatically. But the panick-stricken face of Jodie Chen across the office bullpen had him now running toward another explosion.

"Jodie, what do you need?" His voice rose as he came out from behind his desk. His K-9 partner, Cleo, jumped up and followed. Cleo was a yellow Labrador who had been with him for the last six years of his military duty. She specialized in explosives detection, particularly underwater bombs.

"I had an appointment with a woman in need of protection. She was supposed to be here an hour ago. I think she's in that fire. She's Deaf and might not be able to hear the rescuers. She just video-called me, but all I could see was smoke. I have to go over there, but I need a handler. Tyson would never let me go alone. I'm an admin, not an officer."

"Then let's go. I'll drive." He reached for his keys and led the way toward the door. He stopped and turned back.

Jodie was gnawing on her lower lip and remained in the same spot. For some reason the woman didn't trust him. Things had been fine the first few days after he'd arrived, but soon after that, Jodie kept her distance, avoided him deliberately.

He'd even brought her daisies as an olive branch. He never saw it again and figured she'd tossed it.

"Jodie, this woman needs help," he said. She couldn't argue with that.

"You're still on probation," she said.

"I don't think she'll care."

Jodie squeezed her beautiful amber-and-brown eyes in indecision, and Victor wished he knew how to relieve her of her doubts in him. All he could do was show her that he could handle this job.

He hoped he could, anyway.

"You can trust me," he said.

She glanced in the direction of her office, but then sighed and took her first steps toward the exit. He was glad to see her drop her animosity toward him for the matter at hand. Together with their K-9s by their sides, they headed out to the private parking garage, which was attached to the unit. The only cars parked were their own. With the dogs loaded in their kennels in the back, Victor turned over the ignition of his K-9 SUV and pulled onto the road with only the smoke as a direction.

Jodie pulled up a map on her phone and watched the sky with a worried expression. "I can't believe Monica's in there. When she called me, all I could see was smoke. I have to let the firemen know that someone's inside. Don't take the highway. It will slow us down." She gave him directions that bypassed the heavy traffic.

Victor had no idea who Monica was, but now wasn't the time to figure that out. Stopping Jodie from harming herself in any way was his only concern. "That is a huge fire. I don't want you anywhere near it. It's too dangerous. I'll go there and tell them about Monica."

Had he really just said that? Had he just volunteered to put himself in the flames again?

Victor blew out a wave of anxiety at the memory of being trapped underwater with flames spreading across the surface and nowhere to break through. He never thought coming to Denver to work in law enforcement would send him right back into an inferno.

"We're almost there," Jodie said, still chewing on her lower lip as she looked at the map, then up to the sky ahead of them. "It's a house on Alameda Avenue, across from the park, I think, and it's completely engulfed. If it's hers, I'm too late." Deep regret threaded her voice.

Cleo huffed from behind him in her cage. She sensed the panic in the car. "You don't know that. Maybe Monica got out before the explosion."

A crowd had amassed in the park across the street. Before he had the SUV in Park, Jodie jumped out and ran up to a fireman who was ushering onlookers away. When she tried to get close to the firemen, she was motioned back as well. Victor parked and exited the SUV and could hear Jodie shouting across the wooden barriers that had been set up.

"I have to talk to someone!" she said.

A fireman setting up the perimeter only nodded and told her to hold on.

"Someone's in there. She's Deaf!"

The fireman shouted, "I need you to step back! If this is a gas leak it could still be dangerous."

Victor went around back to release Cleo on a leash, then approached the fireman and Jodie with his badge visible. "Sir, I'm Officer Abrams of the RMKU. We have reason to believe a woman is inside." Victor turned around just in time to see Jodie run behind the neighbor's house and into the backyard.

"Where is she going?" the fireman shouted.

Victor wondered the same thing. He knew the dangers of running toward the flames and didn't wish that pain on anyone, especially the sweet and bubbly Jodie Chen. "I'll stop her," he shouted and raced toward the heat once again. But before he made it halfway there, Cleo yanked the leash back. He turned to see her eyes wide and dark and knew she wouldn't go forward. Victor didn't blame her and put her back in the SUV to go in without her... even if he was just as scared.

TWO

The blistering-hot fire continued to burn. Its roar blocked out all other sounds except Jodie's inner voice telling her she needed to find Monica. As soon as the fireman had shooed her away without listening to her, she ran to the side of the neighbor's house, looking for someone in charge.

And to see if Monica got out the back.

Jodie prayed for the safety of this woman she had never met. She prayed to God to lead her to help Monica the best way she could. Jodie couldn't see how an administrative assistant who trained a dog to sign could be of any help in this situation, but she always believed God had her right where He wanted her, where He could use her.

And today was no different.

"Lead me, God, and be with me down every path and carry me to the end." It was Jodie's daily prayer, taught to her by her mother. She spoke it and signed it. As the RMKU employee who conducted background checks, Jodie prayed it a lot as she dug down deep into many holes to get to the bottom of a criminal's background. She might not be the handler that ran into danger, but snooping into someone's bank records could also be deemed a dangerous pursuit, even though she never stepped foot from behind her multiple monitors. It could even be seen as the equivalent of entering a fire.

The heat scorched the tips of her black hair with every step she took toward the blaze. When she saw two firefighters coming her way, she moved into the black smoke and out of their view.

Jodie called out, "Monica?" and choked on some inhaled smoke. There was no way she could get any closer.

And no way Monica made it out of that fire alive.

As Jodie shielded her burning eyes, she thought the frames of her eyeglasses might melt. She turned away from the inferno and caught sight of a movement behind a back shed. In the next second, a woman came running out from behind it, toward the neighbor's yard.

It had to be Monica, but it was too smoky to tell.

Suddenly, another person, a tall man dressed in a long, black overcoat, stepped out from behind the shed and went in the same direction.

Until he saw Jodie.

He halted and locked his gaze on her. Then he changed his course and came toward her. When he was only about four feet from her, he stopped. Anger burned in his dark eyes as he towered over her. He had to be over six feet. His hair was as black as his coat, and he had a mutilated cheek, as though he had been burned before. She felt his anger, which seemed as deadly as the fire, as he reached inside his black overcoat and pulled out a gun. He took aim right on her.

"Jodie!" Victor's booming voice carried through the haze and whipping flames. "Jodie, where are you?"

She flinched and took her gaze off the guy to quickly glance in the direction of Victor's voice, but her words stuck in her throat and went unspoken.

A glance back in front of her, and the man was gone—he'd slipped away, back into the black billows of smoke.

Jodie startled at his abrupt departure and eyed the thick

smoke. Could he still see her when she couldn't see him? Would he shoot her now?

Jodie took a step back at the realization she was a sitting duck. She hit something hard and immovable and lifted her hands as she turned around to fight for her life.

Victor nearly had his eyes gauged out. He hoped Jodie hadn't meant to do it. Although, with her cold-shoulder treatment lately, he couldn't be so sure. Dodging to the right and protecting his face, he said, "Whoa, it's me, Victor. What are you doing back here?"

"Victor!" Jodie grabbed hold of his coat, practically clinging to him.

"We need to get out of here before the smoke kills us. Why would you come back here?" He guided her out, noticing how she kept looking over her shoulder.

"I think I saw Monica running out from behind the shed, but…" She swallowed hard. "It's probably nothing."

"But what? Jodie, you're shaking. What did you see?" He wrapped his arm tighter around her trembling shoulders and pulled her closer into his chest. If he had to scoop her up, he would. She would hate it, but he didn't care. It wouldn't be the first person he rescued who'd tried to take him down while he did it.

But what did she need rescuing from?

"You can trust me," he said as they walked down the neighbor's side yard.

The uncertain look she sent his way hurt more than he would admit. At some point in the last three weeks, he'd wronged this woman. He led her to his SUV, where Cleo was still crated in the back. Standing at the passenger-side door, she scanned the crowd of onlookers, darting from one cluster to another. She stopped on Victor's face, and the fear in her eyes was unmistakable. She saw something for sure.

Jodie pressed her lips tight then whispered, "Monica was running from somebody. She got out, but there was a man going after her. Victor, I saw him. And when he saw me, he pulled out a gun to shoot me. Right there. If you hadn't called out my name, I might not be alive right now."

Victor exhaled deeply and stopped himself from enveloping her into his arms like a cocoon. "Can you ID him?"

"Y-yes. He couldn't have been more than four feet away from me. Victor…" She swallowed hard again, and he thought she might cry. He placed his palm on one of her pale cheeks. She put her hand over his and held tight. "He looked so angry at me. Like he hated me."

Now Victor *did* pull her close while he scanned the crowd over her silky hair. If a bullet was coming her way, it would have to go through him first. "I need to get you out of here," he whispered, for her ears only. "You can ID him now. It's not safe for you to be out in the open." He opened her car door and guided her inside. "Stay low. I need to inform the police here that there's more to this fire, and Monica is being chased by a possible killer."

Jodie's eyes flitted about the crowd as she crouched down in her seat. "We have to find her before he does."

"You don't have to do any such thing. You've risked too much already." The realization that she could have been shot at point-blank range hit him. "I won't let him hurt you," he promised, knowing that quitting the job was out of the question for now. Whether she liked it or not, he would be sticking to her like glue. He wouldn't leave her even to walk over to the police on the scene.

Victor waved to a Denver PD officer to grab his attention. When the man approached him, Victor explained the situation, and the officer alerted his team to be looking for the gunman.

The officer asked, "Are you leaving?"

Victor looked to Jodie, who had slunk low in the passenger seat. "I need to get her out of here, plus, I'm still a probie." *And haven't been authorized to do anything but fetch coffee yet.* He kept that annoying detail to himself. "But if you need an eyewitness, you know where to find her."

"Good enough." The officer nodded toward Jodie. "Keep her safe."

"I plan to."

Victor climbed in behind the wheel as Jodie said, "I need to call Tyson. He'll know what to do." Her determined words cut him deep.

"So do I," he said, shutting the door a little too hard. "You would know that if Tyson would allow me to have a case every now and then."

THREE

When Victor pulled into the secure RMKU parking garage, Jodie finally breathed a deep sigh of relief.

"You're safe," Victor said, pulling into a spot and securing the SUV. "No one can get in here without access granted."

"I know. I set up the system." Her response came out a little too curt, but she blamed it on her nerves.

"You're amazing at your job," he responded in kind, which only made her feel worse.

She took a deep breath and blew it out. "I should have stayed behind my monitors. My job isn't to help civilians. It's to help the team. That man was so angry. Now I've made things worse. What was I thinking?"

Jodie had spent the whole drive back watching her side mirror to be sure they weren't being tailed.

Would the man come after her, or would he stay on Monica?

Oh, Monica. The woman needed help. It was a matter of life and death. Jodie saw that firsthand.

"You were thinking with your heart, and there's nothing wrong with that. Sometimes that's all we can do."

Jodie glanced his way and wondered if he was speaking about the newspaper article about him. She couldn't ask without alerting him that she'd found it.

Clearing her throat, she nodded toward the other two official vehicles, one RMKU and one FBI, now in the garage. On the way here, she'd called Tyson to fill him in, and he'd assured her he'd meet her at headquarters. "Tyson and the FBI special agent in charge, Michael Bridges, are here already." The RMKU had been created to assist the FBI with difficult cases across the Rocky Mountain region. Jodie was grateful to have both chiefs awaiting them.

She felt better knowing her boss would handle this expertly. Until she knew if the article on Victor was legitimate, she thought it best to limit her trust in his methods.

It was the burden that came with being the one to know everything. Sometimes she wished she could rebury some of the things her research unearthed. There was a fine line between knowing pertinent details and invading someone's privacy. Especially when she wanted to believe they were better than what her background checks pulled up.

"That's great of them to come in so close to Christmas Eve, but I really could have figured this case out. I do have twelve years as a navy SEAL under my belt."

She pushed her glasses up on her nose. "I know you do, but Tyson hasn't released you from your probation yet. Thank you for your willingness, but Tyson and Bridges will take it from here."

As she opened the door to step out, he said, "Did I wrong you in some way?"

With one leg out, she stopped and considered her words. "No, of course not." *It's just that I know something about you that no one knows. Not even Tyson. Because if he did, he would have never hired you.*

Victor held her gaze. "Why am I here, Jodie? I'm beginning to wonder if this move had been a mistake. Maybe I should just go back to New Mexico."

No. She bit her tongue, was conflicted as to what she

should say. She didn't want him to leave, but at the same time, she had to be sure about him before he took on any cases.

She stepped out fully. "Can we talk about this later? I need to fill Tyson in. Monica still needs our help. *If* I can even find her. I need to be in front of my computer." She circled to the back to retrieve Shiloh. Victor did the same for his partner, Cleo.

The two dogs sidled up to each other, their tails wagging with excitement. Cleo was six years older than Shiloh, but her sweet temper seemed to calm Shiloh and put a little assertiveness into his step. Jodie wondered if a mature and wiser K-9 was all Shiloh needed to learn not to hesitate.

"Come," Jodie said and signed the command to them both. The dogs followed as they all entered the headquarters building. Thankfully, Tyson and SAC Bridges were already at her computer, likely pulling up data on Monica Malone.

Tyson glanced up at her when she walked across the wood floor of her small office and approached her desk. His black hair, longer on top, fell across his forehead as he stood, all the while studying her with his intense eyes so dark, they appeared black.

"I'm all right," she said before he asked. "Monica's my main concern right now."

"And you're mine," he said quickly. "You shouldn't have rushed into that situation." He sighed, then quickly reached for her hand to squeeze. "But I'm grateful you're back unscathed."

Jodie felt her lips tremble and tears start to fill her eyes. She took a deep breath to control the response, but she had never been so grateful to work for such a noble man. He released her, and she stepped back. "Thank you, Tyson. That means a lot. I should have called you right away. I'm sorry."

Victor huffed behind her. It was barely a sound, and she

was probably the only one who heard it, but the message was loud and clear.

She was ignoring the fact that he had been helpful at the scene. She couldn't deny that her treatment of him came off as unfair, but she couldn't help her reaction. Not until she knew the truth of what he had done.

She took her seat and realized her last search on him was still open, and Victor Abrams's name was printed on the file tab.

Jodie moved quickly to close it. Victor didn't see it, but Tyson and SAC Bridges most definitely had.

Suddenly, Tyson's words about her being his main concern took on a whole new meaning. Had he read about the incident she'd uncovered about Victor? Did the sergeant know people had died because of him? And, most importantly, would Tyson accuse her of withholding background information from him?

"Special Agent in Charge Michael Bridges," said the FBI man, who was dressed in an impeccable tailored gray suit. He stepped toward Victor and held out his hand to shake. "You can call me SAC Bridges."

"Yes, sir. Victor Abrams. I've heard all about you," Victor said, taking the man's hand. His strong handshake left no doubt about his capabilities. "It's nice to finally meet you."

Jodie had given him some details about the FBI agent from the Denver office, including that he had recently approved the future of RMKU after its probationary period.

"You and I are going to have a talk soon," Bridges informed him. Victor had also heard that the man could be blunt and come off as a little gruff.

Victor liked him. "You remind me of my commander in the navy. He didn't mince words, either."

The special agent's brown eyes squinted. He had very

short brown hair and was probably only a few years older than Victor, but the way he lifted his chin, as though he was sizing him up, reminded Victor they weren't friends.

It also made Victor wonder if he had already insulted the man.

"Sir, if we can put our conversation on hold, I would appreciate it. I fear Jodie is in more danger than she's letting on. She's leaving out an important detail that she was nearly killed." He explained what Jodie saw and how the man pointed a gun at her. "She can ID him. That explosion was no accident. and this guy is not going to be happy at being seen. My gut tells me he's coming after her."

SAC Bridges turned to face Jodie. "Jodie, I'm sure I don't have to remind you how we need all the details to be able to carry out our work fully and safely for the whole team."

Jodie visibly swallowed and pushed up her glasses on her nose. "Absolutely. But right now, I need to focus on Monica." She glanced at Victor, then back at the screen in front of her. "I know the best place I can help her is at my computer."

Bridges nodded. "And that's why you're the best at your job. We trust you. Both Tyson and I know you have the team's best interests at heart. We hope you understand that includes you."

"Yes, sir."

"And you can come to us. With anything. You don't have to bear the responsibility alone. We want you safe, both outside the office, as well as in."

Victor felt there was more to this conversation than he was privy to. Like they were referencing him. Did they think he would harm her in some way?

He sputtered at the idea. He wouldn't harm a single hair on her beautiful head. The idea that Jodie believed otherwise made it feel as though he'd just taken a kick to the ribs.

Jodie's phone rang, and as she glanced at it, her eyes widened. "It's Monica. Oh, thank God. She's alive." Jodie hit the answer button and on the computer screen, the woman's face filled the monitor. Terror-stricken eyes grabbed everyone's attention. Monica began to sign, as did Jodie.

"Where are you?" Jodie spoke with her hands but also said the words out loud, for the benefit of the others. "We will come get you right now."

The woman signed as Jodie translated. "'Too late. No time. He's here.'"

Jodie replied, "Where is here? Where are you?"

As Jodie signed with the woman, Tyson used another monitor to try and trace the call. SAC Bridges came around the back of Jodie's chair.

"She looks to be in some sort of old factory," Victor said, seeing tall windows surrounded by brick.

Tyson said, "Ask her if she'll move to a window. But stay low. Maybe we can get a location if we see a familiar land marker outside."

Jodie signed his request, but Monica shook her head, seemingly frightened at the idea. She looked over her shoulder and signed something.

Jodie translated the signs, saying, "'I had to say something. I don't regret it.'"

Then Monica signed what looked like some letters. Victor recognized them as such but didn't know sign language well enough to decipher them. He'd only recently started studying the language on his own after watching Jodie train Shiloh.

Then a man appeared behind Monica.

Tyson raced to track the location of the call while Jodie tapped the keys on her keyboard to capture the man's face.

Suddenly the screen went black.

"Got it," Tyson said.

"Got it," Jodie said at the same time. "And it's the same man I saw at the fire." As she stared at the screenshot, Victor watched her visibly tremble.

SAC Bridges tapped Jodie on the shoulder. "Fast work. Nice job. I'll run that image to see if we can match it to any facial recognitions on file. Tyson, I'll get a team over there right now." He turned away with his phone to start giving orders.

Victor said, "I'm going." He would not be sitting this case out.

Victor and Tyson looked at Jodie. She looked at her computer.

"What are you all keeping from me?" Victor leaned down and put his hands on the desk, searching her computer screens for the answer.

Tyson replied, "After this is all done, I'll be asking you the same question."

FOUR

"Can we just focus on Monica right now?" Jodie said quickly, attempting to hold off this conversation for the time being. "She needs us." She sent pleading eyes toward Tyson.

At his short nod, she breathed a sigh of relief. As bad as the article painted Victor, she was surprised at the hope she still held out with regard to him. She told herself that it was only fair until she had something concrete, but deep down she wondered if it was more personal.

As Tyson and SAC Bridges went to work organizing a team to head to the location, Jodie shut down her monitors and came out from behind her desk. She signed to Shiloh to come. "I need some fresh air. Victor, I would appreciate if you stayed behind with me. We can head out to the training yard with the dogs."

His jaw ticked with obvious annoyance at being cut out of the case as he looked from her to Tyson. "Fine. But I'd like to be kept up-to-date on what's found at the factory."

"Keep your phone on," Tyson said as he headed toward the exit, then called his own K-9 from his office.

When the department settled into a heavy silence with her and Victor and their two dogs, he looked at her intensely. "I want to know what's going on."

"I can't share that right now. It would be a breach of my job."

He tilted his head, eyeing her suspiciously. "And all I want to do *is* my job. But it appears it's you who has been standing in the way of that. I have a right to know why."

She glanced at her black screen, which moments ago had had the *Mariana Islands Daily News* article opened. "I found something." She frowned.

"On me?" He looked at her screen as well, but he gave no answers. "You ran my background check and security checks. I wouldn't be here if they hadn't panned out."

"I found an opinion piece. That's why it's not in your files. It didn't come up in your checks. It didn't come up until I…"

"Until you what?"

This was another reason why Jodie had kept what she'd found to herself. She didn't want to have to admit to Tyson that she had been doing a web search on Victor for personal reasons. And she definitely didn't want to admit that to Victor. The truth was, the day he walked into the office for the first time, she liked him.

"When you arrived on that first day, you were telling me about where you were stationed. My grandfather had his medical practice on Guam after he left Taiwan."

"I remember the conversation. What about it?"

"After you left, I searched online about your station." She glanced at Shiloh, who was waiting for her by the door. "Can we hold off on this conversation, please? Once I do a little more investigation, I'm sure you'll be cleared to work."

"I don't understand what has to be cleared? I was honorably discharged."

Jodie bit her lower lip in indecision. "There seems to be some discrepancy about an incident that happened on a yacht off the coast. That's all I'm going to say about it.

Now if you'll excuse me, I'm going out to the training yard. I need some fresh air. This has been a really traumatic day for me."

She swept past him and could see the color in his face draining. He looked guilty, and that only made her feel worse. She had been hoping the article had been a mistake. This was one of those times she wished she didn't know everything about someone. Ignorance really could be bliss.

Long after the back door to the training yard closed, Victor was still standing in the middle of Jodie's office. She was good. Real good.

He had been assured that the incident wouldn't taint his future. That all evidence of it had been wiped from his files. He didn't know how she found out, or why, but it didn't matter now. What mattered was she knew, and soon, so would Tyson.

Victor headed out of Jodie's office and toward his desk in the bullpen. His days here were numbered. Thankfully, he hadn't accumulated too much in his short time at the RMKU. It wouldn't take him long to pack up. He piled a few of his books on the side of the desk and opened an empty file cabinet for some snacks he had stashed in there. He went to the lounge and grabbed a small box from inside the counter. He brought it back to his desk and filled it with his meager belongings, stacking the books on top.

Then his phone alerted him to a message. A quick glance and he saw it was Tyson.

Two sentences scrawled across the screen. We found Monica's body. Guard Jodie.

Victor touched the box with one hand and held his phone in the other. He considered it ironic that Tyson would give him a responsibility in the moment he was walking out the door.

He responded to Tyson. I'm sorry to hear that. I'll inform Jodie. This will crush her.

Knowing this made Victor realize leaving wasn't possible just yet. Whether Jodie wanted his protection or not, he was all she had at the moment. There was no doubt in his mind that the man who killed Monica would be coming for Jodie next.

If something happened to her… *No*, he wouldn't leave her unprotected. He would never leave his partner again.

Taking Cleo, he headed to the back door to the training yard. He stepped out and stood back for a few moments to watch her work with Shiloh. It was how he'd first met her. She had been out back here teaching the dog sign language. They struck up a conversation on how her mom, Suki Chen, was Deaf and how she had grown up as a military kid stationed on Guam with her family. It was how her mother had met her future husband. They married and returned to the States to live and raise their own family.

Victor had found Jodie's bubbly personality and joy in her work so attractive. He found the woman even more so. He was pretty sure that Tyson would frown upon an office romance, but that didn't stop Victor from being intrigued by her. Within a couple of days, however, her cold shoulder had told him it didn't matter, anyway. She didn't feel the same way.

"Jodie, I need to talk with you," he said to her back. She immediately stiffened at the sound of his voice, and that only made him feel worse. He hoped someday, he could explain, if he could rationalize that whole incident himself, but for now, her safety was all that mattered.

She turned to face him. "What is it?"

There was no easy way to say this. "Monica's dead. Tyson just texted me and said they found her body."

Jodie's face crumpled instantly. "No," she said on a suppressed wail, covering her mouth.

Victor rushed to her, his arms out, and made contact with her shoulders. "You have to listen to me. There is nothing you could have done. Don't take this blame on. Trust me, it will eat at you if you do. Are you listening to me?" He nearly shook her. "Don't take this blame on."

"How can I not? She reached out to me for help. I failed her." Suddenly, she stepped back to go around him. "I have to go there. Right now." She reached the door, just as he went after her, staying in step with her.

"You can't go. It's not safe for you to be out there. Tyson wants me to guard you."

"I'm going." She reached for the doorknob.

Victor put his hand on the door to hold it closed. "The killer would come after you. You can ID him."

She chewed on her lower lip in indecision—the war going on within her was clearly etched on her face. Facing him, she said, "I have to see her." Her liquid brown-and-amber eyes implored him to do something.

Victor swallowed convulsively. He could be making the biggest mistake ever. Bigger than what happened in the Mariana Islands. Because with Jodie, he knew the danger he was running into. "I will take you. I just hope I don't regret this as well."

FIVE

Jodie led Shiloh back out to the parking garage. As she approached her little car, she realized they couldn't take both dogs. She came to an abrupt stop and turned back to Victor, who was leading Cleo beside him. "We have to take your SUV. I don't typically transport the K-9s, and we won't all fit."

"We could leave the dogs in the kennel."

"There's not time," Jodie said.

Suddenly, Cleo began barking and moved in a circle. Victor looked at her car and quickly scanned the parking garage, maneuvering himself to be on the other side of Jodie, and then he backed her toward his car. "Get in my car," he said. "Cleo's sensing something. Someone's been in here. They still might be."

He pushed the key fob and unlocked his car doors. Jodie climbed into the front seat of the SUV and watched as he approached her vehicle slowly. Scanning inside the passenger-side window, he shook his head before returning to his own car and loading the dogs.

"What is it?" she asked, once he sat behind the wheel.

"Your glove compartment has been rummaged through. Whoever it was knows where you live now. He's found you. I really don't think you should be going downtown. It's not safe."

"Victor, this garage was the safest place for me to be, so really, no place is safe. He got through my wall. What am I supposed to do? I can't even go home now."

"You're right." He took a deep breath and looked in his rearview mirror. He started the ignition, mumbling that he was going to regret this.

"I'm going with or without you," she said. "I owe it to Monica to be there."

He backed out of the parking spot and said, "I have to disagree. You don't owe anybody anything. Is this why you train Shiloh?"

"What's that supposed to mean?" she asked, affronted.

"That dog failed the assessment. Any smart handler would let him go and be someone's pet. The fact that you can't let him go tells me you you want to save the day for everyone."

Jodie sputtered. "That's not fair. I see the good in people and in dogs and I root for them. What's wrong with that?"

"Nothing's wrong with it until someone ends up dead because of it." He drove through the garage and out to the street in silence as Jodie wondered if he was on to something. He was correct in his thinking about how she rooted for the underdog. But she wasn't about to admit that to him.

"Well, don't worry about me. I've seen the team work long enough to know the ropes."

He huffed as he drove on toward downtown and the industrial section. "Knowing the ropes isn't enough. Those ropes can tangle you up if not used correctly and responsibly."

She wanted to tell him that she wasn't his responsibility. Then he pulled up to the factory with all the RMKU and FBI vehicles, and the coroner's van out front. Suddenly, she could feel those ropes tightening around her.

A killer wanted her dead. Avoiding that truth only put her further in harm's way.

* * *

Victor was livid about Jodie's car being broken into, but he was glad to see her being wise and staying in the car with him. He texted Tyson to let him know they were there, and to make plans to have her car processed for prints. She cleared her throat and looked uneasy. Not that he blamed her. This whole situation had put them both on edge.

"We'll find him. He's bound to mess up. All we need is one print." Victor did his best to assure her but sounded like he was only trying to assure himself.

"You mentioned something back at headquarters about regret." She wrung her hands in her lap, and he knew how she was feeling.

He leaned over and reached her hands. "Hey, you have nothing to regret. You did everything you could and more."

Facing him, she asked, "Did you?"

"Did I what?" Suddenly, Victor felt the conversation take 180-degree turn.

"Whatever it is that you regretted. Did you do everything you could…and more?"

A flash of burning flames spreading out on the ocean water above him came to mind. He nodded. "I tried, but I wasn't fast enough."

"I'm assuming this is the incident on the Mariana Islands?" When he didn't answer, she asked, "The article said an islander died. And that you were to blame."

"I suppose they would see it that way." Victor stared off at the law-enforcement vehicles and beyond. He could see there was an alley between the factory building and the other one next to it. "The woman who died was the daughter of a prominent figure on the island. She was kidnapped for ransom and was being kept on a yacht at sea. When my partner and I boarded, we found her locked in a room. She told us there was a bomb on the boat's hull. My partner wanted us to work on getting the door open and getting her out. But I left with Cleo to find the underwater explosive. Defusing was my specialty. I thought I could find the bomb and give them more time to get out. When I finally found it, or I should say Cleo found it, I could see there was less than a minute left. I had no time to alert him to get off the boat." He pressed his lips tight. "I left my partner behind, and the woman we were supposed to be saving."

Jodie sat still for an extended held breath. Then he heard her let it go. "What part of that do you regret?"

"Perhaps if I had stayed on board and worked with my partner to get that door open, they would both be alive today. I guess the people of the island thought so, too. I hadn't realized someone wrote an article about me." He glanced off again, this time catching a movement in the alley. A shadow, he thought, but it moved.

"What I need to know is do you regret leaving your partner behind?" she asked while he scanned the alley. The shadow was now gone. "Victor, answer me. I need to know."

He opened the car door. "Don't get out of the car. Lock up behind me. I'll be right back." He ran at full speed toward the alley. When he reached it, he looked down into the darkness and readied his sidearm. The corridor appeared empty, but he stepped into it and made his way to the other side.

He came out on a courtyard and scanned the walkways for that dark figure he knew he'd seen. By the time he made it across the courtyard and down another alley, it dawned on him that he'd just left Jodie and the K-9s behind. He turned back on a run, realizing he'd failed to protect his team again.

SIX

Jodie sat in stunned silence long after Victor had run from the car. She had known from the article that he had been blamed for the death of the woman, but she didn't know he had left a team member behind. The opinion piece had reported a military death as well, but the journalist must not have known how it happened. But now she did, and Tyson needed to know before Victor received any cases.

She picked up her phone to text Tyson. When she saw the time on her phone, she realized Victor had been gone for a while.

Too long.

She looked out the window to search the direction he had gone. With no sign of him, she looked to the law-enforcement vehicles, and saw no one around. Suddenly, Jodie realized she was all alone. Getting out of the car didn't seem wise, but neither did sitting here and waiting for Victor to return.

What if he was hurt?

She shook her head. That was part of the job. She didn't run off and help the handlers if they got themselves in a situation. She was strictly an admin. The only thing she could do was pray.

Bowing her head, she asked God to give her some direction. Should she stay and wait for Victor or go inside the factory and see Tyson? She knew if she went inside, she would tell him all Victor had confided to her. Knowing that she should, as one of her responsibilities to her boss, should have propelled her, but instead she stayed seated.

Someone must've thought Victor was not responsible because charges hadn't been brought against him. It might have just been a poor choice that he'd made. She reasoned that she should talk to him more about it first. Then his accusation of her having to save everybody came back. Was she doing it again with him?

Jodie dropped her head into her hands and groaned in indecision. She looked at her phone and saw more time had lapsed. Did the man not realize he had just left her behind when his orders were to guard her? This only made her want to contact Tyson right then and there.

She flung open the door. "That's it." She wasn't waiting another second for the man to return. She was going inside to help her boss and inform him about the new recruit.

She made her way to the entrance of the factory, weaving through the vehicles. When she reached the door, she looked in the direction of the alley that Victor had gone down. She bypassed the door and walked over, peering down the alley.

"Victor?" she called, her voice echoing.

When no response came, she shook her head and headed back toward the door of the factory. She took out her phone and started to call Tyson.

In the next second, something looped around her neck, yanking her backward. She dropped the phone, and heard it hit the pavement as she clutched at some kind of thin plastic choking her. She had no room to move as her back pushed against a hard chest. She felt her feet lift off the ground, and all she could do was kick useless air. She couldn't get a foothold or anything to brace herself against.

Her lungs squeezed in pain as she couldn't take in any

air. Her mind raced with a will to survive and a need for oxygen. Stars and flashing lights clouded her vision as she felt her arms go limp.

The flashes stopped, and so did her fight.

Victor raced out of the alleyway to get back to Jodie. Just as he stepped out to the parking lot, he tripped at the sight he came upon. He couldn't see much, except for her short legs dangling as a man in a black overcoat had her pulled close to him.

Victor didn't think twice. He picked up his speed and barreled straight toward the man, knocking him right to the ground. But that also meant Jodie went flying with him. In an instant, the thug bolted for the alley, his black coat whipping behind him.

On his knees, Victor scrambled over to her where her body lay unmoving. He scooped her up into his arms, then tapped her cheeks and listened for any breathing.

"Jodie, Jodie, wake up. Please, wake up." He watched as her head lolled to the right and fell against his chest. She was still alive. He breathed a sigh of relief. He thought about giving her some of his own breath, but she inhaled sharply, and her eyes flashed wide.

Struggling in his arms, he held her tight. "You're okay. It's me, Victor. You're safe."

"What…happened?" she croaked out.

"I left you too long. It won't happen again. I went after the man, but he must have ducked behind something and come after you after I passed him. I'm so sorry. How is your breathing?" He watched as color flooded back into her face and her breathing returned to normal. He realized his grip was too tight and loosened his hold on her small frame. He didn't want to hurt her in his panic.

In one swift movement, he stood and kept her close in his arms. "I need to get you out of here."

Her wide, frightened eyes watched him intently. He noticed her glasses were askew on her face and he reached one hand up to straighten them for her. "Where will I go?" He could tell she was struggling a bit to speak. "Nowhere is safe."

As he carried her back to the car, she craned her neck to look behind her. "My phone. I dropped it."

"I'll get it in a moment. First I'm putting you into the car." Once he had her situated and the door closed securely, he went back and found her cracked phone. Pushing the button, he could see it still worked. Just then, a text came in and it dinged in his hand. He brought the phone back to her door and opened it to pass it over. "You've got a text."

Jodie sighed at seeing the crack but read the message. "It's my friend Daniella. She used to be a handler for the RMKU. But she married and moved to New Mexico. Silver City. It looks like she already heard about the incident this morning and is checking in with me." Jodie texted back her friend as Victor texted the latest event to Tyson.

Soon after sending the text, Tyson came out of the factory, straight for the car. He stood beside him outside the passenger window. "Are you all right?" he asked Jodie.

She nodded to him but rubbed her throat. "It hurts still, but I'll be okay."

Tyson looked to Victor. "Monica was strangled as well. Some sort of electrical wire was used. Particularly, a wire for an explosive, like a car bomb."

Victor shot a glance Jodie's way. "Jodie's car was broken into in the parking garage. I want the car processed for prints, but if this guy is making car bombs, approach carefully. Now that I think about it, Cleo had been acting strange around it. I should have realized she might have detected explosives. It's her specialty."

"I'll proceed with caution," Tyson said. "But right now,

I need to know where you can take Jodie. She's our main concern."

Jodie held up her phone. "Daniella says I can come stay at her lodge in New Mexico. She and her husband and son are away. I know where the key is."

Tyson looked to Victor. "You up for a ride? It's about eleven hours."

"I can handle it." Victor made his way around the front of the SUV and climbed in behind the wheel.

Jodie pushed up in her seat. "Wait. I didn't say he could come with me." She kept her eyes on her boss, looking away from Victor. "I think we should talk about this. There are things you need to know."

Tyson shook his head. "There's no time. I don't even want you going back to your apartment. Get on the road and buy what you need as you drive farther away. I'll re-imburse you."

"This isn't about money. This is about safety. And trust." Jodie turned to look at him.

Victor could tell she wanted to share about the Mari-ana Islands with her boss. He knew that it was inevitable, but right now her safety was all that mattered. "You can trust me. Plus, there is no way I'm leaving your side now. Whether I'm a handler, or not."

Tyson sent him a warning glare. "If anything happens to her, I will hold you accountable."

Victor nodded once. "I don't want it any other way."

"Can either of you let me make this decision on my own?" Jodie said with frustration in her voice.

"What do you have in mind?" Victor asked genuinely. He waited for her to give her input. "You're one of the smartest people I know. If you have a better idea of where you can go, just say so."

"I want to go to Daniella's. I don't want to go to my

mom's house and bring her danger. I just don't understand why you have to go."

Victor felt a stab of rejection cut straight through his chest and prick his heart. So this was about him. "Please don't put yourself in jeopardy because you feel you have to refuse my help. Right now, with everyone out of the office on cases or for Christmas, there is no one else to take you. Not if we need to get on the road right away. Let me help you."

Jodie leaned back and glanced up at Tyson's expectant face. At his nod, she sighed her agreement. "Fine. I'm too tired to fight, anyway."

With that, Tyson went back to work, and Victor started the engine and headed out toward the highway. With an eleven-hour drive ahead of them, he stopped for a coffee two towns over and went through the drive-through. When he pulled up, he turned to Jodie to ask if she wanted something, but she was already sound asleep.

It was just as well. Eleven hours of her sleeping was better than eleven hours of the silent treatment.

Victor didn't know what else he could say to fix what was wrong between them. Jodie had already made up her mind about him, and there was nothing he could do to change that.

An hour into the drive, Tyson called to inform him that a car bomb had been found in the Jodie's car. If she had started that engine, she would have been dead.

SEVEN

Jodie slowly came out of her slumber, and with groggy eyes looked at the change of scenery. It was drastically different from Denver—sand and red rocks filled her vision.

"Welcome back, sleepyhead," Victor said from the driver seat.

She looked his way. "Monica was trying to tell me something." She grabbed the top of her head as she racked her brain for the memory. "I just dreamt about her, but I can't remember what she was signing."

"If I remember correctly and if I have this right, I think they were letters. But that's as much as I can help you. I'm still learning the language. But now that you're awake, we need to talk about your car."

"What about it? And why are you learning sign language?"

"It was rigged, just as I thought. And to train Cleo, like you're training Shiloh. The military chose to retire her, but I know she still has years left in her. She struggles with fire now, but perhaps helping the Deaf can be her new specialty."

Jodie looked back at the dogs and signed "I love you." Their ears perked up and their eyes brightened. "She understands. She'll learn quick." Turning back with a smile, Jodie let her head fall back to the headrest. Then her thoughts drifted back to her dream and Monica's killer, and she let her smile go. "He tried to kill me, too."

"Yes. And he's not going to stop until he succeeds."

"If he knew I had his screenshot, perhaps that would make him stop chasing me down. I'm not the only one who can identify him now. The RMKU and the FBI can, too."

"You're grasping at straws. That will only make you lose your focus."

"Right." She sighed. "He wants me dead."

Victor drove on in a heavy silence, glancing in his rear-view mirror repeatedly. After a few minutes, he said, "We need to make a stop here soon with the dogs." He looked at his mirror again, his lips pressed tight in a concerned expression.

"Is something wrong?" she asked.

"Just being cautious. We've been on the road now for five hours, but that doesn't mean we're alone."

Jodie looked behind her at the headlights of numerous cars in rush-hour traffic. Any one of them could be the killer, or not. "Maybe get off the exit, and we'll find a res-taurant. If we're being followed, we'll know right away."

"Maybe." He changed lanes at the last second and took the exit all in one move. If someone was following them, he'd given them no time to move over.

With the setting sun, the roads were getting dark, and so were their surroundings. He pulled into a diner and parked around back. He shut the lights off, and they sat for a few minutes to see if anyone would come.

"Looks clear to me," Jodie said. She glanced in the back of the SUV. "May I use your laptop to do a little research? I'll use my phone's hot spot for Wi-Fi."

Victor reached behind him for the bag and passed it over to her. She powered up, and he put in his passcode for her to start her search. "Are you hungry?" he asked.

Jodie felt her throat where the wire had squeezed. "I

am, but something soft." She glanced his way and saw him frowning in the lights of the dashboard. "Hey, I got out of your SUV. You told me to stay, and I didn't. I have some blame, too."

"All right, let me take the dogs out for a few minutes, in sight of my vehicle, and then we'll go inside to get something to eat."

As Victor attended to the dogs, Jodie searched for details about Monica online. She wondered who this man was to her. A disgruntled partner? An abusive spouse? Jodie looked up her marital status and found that she was not married. But it still could be an abusive boyfriend.

Thinking back to the video call, Victor said he definitely saw Monica signing letters, but what were they? Jodie had been so focused on getting the screenshot of the killer that she'd missed what Monica was telling her.

More guilt flooded in. She really messed up with this woman.

Victor opened the driver's door. "The dogs can come in with us. They even have some dog treats inside. Let's go get a bite to eat."

Jodie closed the laptop and put it back in the bag. She made her way around the back of the car and came up alongside Victor and the dogs. They walked together into the restaurant and chose one of the empty booths at the back. They could watch the car from the window.

"Oh, cute dogs!" the waitress said as she came over in a blue dress and apron. She reached inside the apron and brought out two dog bones. "May I give them to them?"

"We have to feed it to them," Victor said. "They're working dogs and can only take it from the handler."

Jodie signed "sit" to them both to wait for their treat, then said to Victor, "Cleo really is taking to sign language quickly. I'm impressed."

The waitress passed the small dog bones to Victor, and

he gave them to the excited dogs. "That is so neat," she said, taking out her notepad for their order. "I didn't realize dogs could understand sign language."

Victor pored over a menu. "We're working on it. I think my dog is catching on faster than I am."

Jodie rubbed her throat, which was still sore from being choked. "I would just like some soup," she said without opening her menu. She hoped it would be soothing.

"All we have is chicken noodle tonight," the waitress informed her.

Victor closed his menu. "I'll have the chicken soup, too." He collected Jodie's menu and passed them both back to the waitress. "And coffee, please."

Once the waitress walked away, Jodie said to him, "You didn't have to order soup just because of me. I'm sure you would much rather have a big burger, or something. You've been driving all afternoon."

He tapped his fingers on the table in front of him. "I like soup, too. I find it comforting. Right now, I could use some comfort."

She looked at her own hands and wondered if his nervousness had something to do with how she had found the article. "Are you worried about losing the job?"

He shrugged. "I'm more worried about keeping you alive. I can always find another position." He toyed with the napkin to his left, and after a few moments he scrunched it up in his fist, then flattened it out. He seemed more upset than he was letting on.

"You know I have to do my job." Jodie leaned forward over the table.

Slowly, Victor leaned in as well. Their faces were less than a foot apart. "So do I," he said quietly.

The waitress stepped up with two bowls. "Aw, isn't this sweet. Hate to interrupt you two but here are your bowls of soup." She placed them down between them.

Both Victor and Jodie leaned back in their seats, fidgeting at what they might've just looked like to the waitress. She must have thought they were on a date.

The waitress slipped away but returned quickly with a coffee pot. This time the two of them sat straighter in their seats as she turned over their cups on their saucers. "Is there anything else I can get you?" she asked as she poured two steaming cups and slid them over.

At the shake of their heads, she went away again. Once they were alone again, Jodie brought the conversation back to figuring out who this man was to Monica. "He could be her boyfriend. Or had been her boyfriend." Jodie frowned.

Victor nodded to her soup. "Eat while it's warm." He picked up his own spoon to show her and dug in.

She did the same, realizing how hungry she was. When she finished, she looked up and found him smiling at her.

"Do you feel better?" he asked.

"I'll feel better when I know who this guy is and why he was after Monica. And why he's after me now."

"Same. Because he's so relentless in his pursuit of you, just because you can identify him, tells me that what Monica had on him was bad. Either she could identify him for something, or she knew he was up to something no good. He must think you know what that is."

"Right. He saw her sign to me. He thinks I know." She groaned and dropped her head into her hands. "I wish I could remember."

"Maybe it will come to us."

Jodie downed her coffee. "We should get going. Do you want me to drive for a little while?"

Victor stood up and motioned for the dogs to do the same. "I'm fine. After you." He waved her forward. When they reached the door, she turned back to see he hadn't budged.

"Are you coming?" she asked.

Victor was facing the men's room with his brow furrowed. He shook his head and headed her way. "I thought I saw something."

They stepped outside into the dark night. "What did you see?"

"Someone had gone into the men's room, and I just caught a quick glimpse of a black coat. But that doesn't mean he's the killer."

"Do you want to go check it out?"

"I'm not leaving your side. Let's just go."

After Cleo sniffed for explosives around the vehicle, they all piled back into the SUV. Jodie was appreciative that Victor didn't leave her to go check it out. She just wanted to get back on the road and get to Daniella's lodge.

As they headed back out to the highway, she watched Victor keep his eyes on his mirrors. After about ten minutes of his intense scrutiny, she said, "We're being followed, aren't we?"

"Yeah." He switched lanes and passed a tractor-trailer truck, speeding up. "Things could get bumpy. Stay buckled. I'll get us out of this... I hope."

Nearly six hours passed, and Victor was fairly certain he'd lost their tail. They were almost at the lodge, but he still hesitated driving directly there. They'd left the highway a while ago and were now driving through mountain roads leading into Silver City. The forest of Gila Wilderness National Monument land surrounded them. Victor knew from growing up in New Mexico that the monument consisted of steep cliff dwellings, and he would have to pay attention on these dark roads. He hadn't seen another car in miles.

Glancing to his right, he saw Jodie's eyes were closed. "Are you awake?" he asked softly.

"Yes. I'm just trying to remember what those letters

were that Monica signed." She sounded so forlorn. "I think it's hopeless. I should give up, but I just can't."

As Victor checked his mirrors, he tried to remember what one of them might have looked like. "I think one might have been twisting two of her fingers together." He removed his right hand to show her.

Jodie sat up quickly. "That's an *R*. Do you remember anything else?"

Victor shook his head. "Maybe a pointed finger?"

She fell back into her seat. "That could be a few different letters."

"I'm sorry I can't be more help."

She waved her hand as she closed her eyes again. "I'll figure it out. It will come to me."

"Can I help with anything else?"

"I have to do this." She turned her face toward the window, effectively shutting him out.

Victor drove on into the darkness, taking the curvy road toward the lodge. An intersection approached ahead, and he slowed down to prepare to stop. He took the moment to discuss the tension between them.

"I know you don't trust me to do this job, and I should have shared about the incident before I came to RMKU. I know that. I guess part of me just wanted to put it behind us."

"Us?"

Victor came to a stop at the intersection and looked to the rear of the SUV. "Cleo was there, too. She was just as traumatized. If not more." As Jodie gazed over her shoulder at the dogs, he continued with his request. "I would like a second chance to start over. I genuinely want to be your friend." There were no other cars waiting to go, so he stayed put to wait for her response.

None came as she faced forward.

Victor looked at his rearview mirror and saw no cars

behind them. To his left, he could see the headlights of one vehicle far off. He continued to wait for her to respond, looking her way. In her silence, he could see she was struggling with her decision.

But at least it wasn't a no…yet.

Reaching over, he took her hand. He was glad to see her not tense up. Maybe there was hope for a friendship with her, after all. "From the day I walked into the RMKU, you have intrigued me," he said. "To watch you at your monitors work so efficiently, always three steps ahead of everybody, put me in awe of how your mind works. You understand strategy, which is something even the strongest of officers often lack. But that doesn't mean you have to face this case alone. Use me. Even just to bounce things off of. You *can* trust me. Let me help you."

Slowly, Jodie turned his way. But before she could say a word, her eyes behind her glasses widened in stark fear. Her mouth gaped open in fright as she locked eyes on something over his shoulder.

Victor turned back to look out his driver's window just as a car with its headlights off smashed into his side door, jerking them with the impact and pushing his SUV toward the Gila Wilderness cliffs. The sound of the crash echoed through his head and his hands vibrated as he gripped the steering wheel tightly.

Victor hit the gas to try to get out from the momentum. But that didn't work, so he put the car into Reverse just as they were about to go over.

There was a loud squealing of tires from both vehicles as he pulled back, and the other car took a hard left and raced up the road, away from them. Victor hit the brakes and brought the SUV to a halt, feeling the shaking aftermath all around him and through him.

It took several moments before he could say a word. Glancing toward Jodie, he saw she was just as stunned.

"I...didn't even see him until he was there," she whispered.

"Are you hurt?" he asked, barely managing to say the words.

She searched his face frantically. "I wasn't the one hit. Are *you* okay?" She looked at his hands and chest, reaching her own hands out to touch his chin.

As Victor's adrenaline eased, he put a hand to his face and felt the sticky wetness of blood dripping down into his collar. The driver's window had been smashed out. "I must have hit my head on it on impact." He felt the side of his head, where a welt was already forming. Pain began to set in, ricocheting through his skull.

"You need to see a doctor."

He shook his head only slightly. "I need to get you to the lodge." He reached for his door handle and saw there was no way the door would open again. He tried to push on it, but that only caused more pain through his head and also in his shoulder. Feeling it, he wondered if it was broken. "We're not far from the lodge." He gritted his teeth. "We'll have to go out your side. But before you open that door and step out, I need to make sure the cliff is not right there. Can you open it carefully?"

As Jodie opened her door slowly, and peered down, she said, "We have a few feet. We're good." She looked behind her. "The dogs are okay. They're looking at us with scared eyes, but they're alert."

"Thank God," he said. And sent up a quick prayer of gratitude and plea for help.

Jodie shot a glance his way. "I didn't know you were a man who prayed."

Victor shrugged, or at least tried to, with only one working shoulder. "I am nothing without Him."

"I feel the same way. My daily prayer is 'lead me, God, and be with me down every path and carry me to the end.'

Whether I'm chasing a trail on the computer, or heading down to the woods to this lodge, I know He'll be with us."

Victor smiled softly at her. "You intrigue me more and more every day." Then he looked behind her at where they had to go. "I hope He's going to carry me, because I don't know how this leg will. My whole left side is screaming in pain." Glancing ahead, he wondered where the driver had gone…and when he would return.

Jodie exited first and did her best to help him climb over her seat. Every movement blinded him with pain, and when he finally stood before her, he was pretty sure she was holding him up. He dropped his head to her forehead and bit back a groan. He felt her rub his back and whisper something, but he couldn't hear anything through the pain.

"Give me a moment," he said. He took a few deep breaths, smelling her sweet, flowery shampoo, and closed his eyes to let everything that was Jodie Chen calm his nerve endings. Slowly, the pain subsided, and he chuckled. "I'm not usually this much of a baby."

She laughed and the sweet, bubbly sound tugged at his heartstrings. "I won't hold it against you. You were just hit head-on."

Victor thought of the first moment he had laid eyes on her when he'd walked into the RMKU three weeks ago. That impact had been just as monumental, if not more.

He pulled back abruptly. "We need to go," he said. The direction his thoughts were headed needed to be cut off at the pass, just as his car had been. A relationship with Jodie would go nowhere, also just like his car. "I'll have to come back for the vehicle or send a tow truck in the morning."

They turned, and Jodie wrapped her arm around his waist as they headed to the rear of the vehicle to release the dogs. She opened the back door and commanded them both to step out and sit.

Cleo did, but Shiloh did not.

Jodie signed and spoke the commands aloud, but Shiloh remained unmoved. "This was why he failed the assessment. He's just too skittish. Come on, Shiloh. I know you have it in you. Come." She reached a hand to him and let him sniff it.

Slowly, Shiloh trembled, but came forward, becoming familiar with his whereabouts. He stepped down cautiously.

Victor frowned. "I should tell you to let him go. He would already be gone in the navy. In a moment of danger, having to coerce him like this puts us at more risk for having him along."

"I don't see it that way. I know you think I want to save the day for everybody and want to save him, but that's not it, either. I want to give him the opportunity to prove that he can be trusted."

As they headed down into the Gila Wilderness that would lead to the lodge, Victor walked beside Jodie and wondered why she couldn't give him the same opportunity.

EIGHT

Sam and Daniella Kavanaugh's remote Cliffside Lodge loomed ahead as Jodie guided Victor down from the edge of the property, and the dogs trounced ahead by a few feet. Jodie's good friend now resided here with her husband and their son, Oliver, only they weren't home, having gone away for the holiday.

"I know where the key is. Daniella told me where to find it." Jodie left Victor by the door with Cleo and took Shiloh with her to the shed. A brick by the door hid the key, and she had it in her hand quickly. She raced back to Victor, hoping she could get him inside to check his wounds before he lost any more blood. Once the door opened, he stumbled a bit with the computer bag over his shoulder. She took it from him and helped him to the couch in the main room. When she moved to turn the lamp on beside him, he grabbed her hand.

"No bright light just yet. I'll get a fire going in a moment," he said. "But let's not bring any attention to ourselves right now."

Jodie found herself lingering for a moment, continuing to hold his hand, as she fought the urge to entwine her fingers into his. To do so would reveal her hidden thoughts that she had worked so hard to push aside. She needed to for the job. The RMKU came first.

"Can I put the computer on?" she asked, and at his nod, she pulled her hand away from his and opened the bag.

"Just keep the screen light down. And stay away from the window."

"I didn't want to put it on to use it. I need some light to see your head. You've lost a lot of blood."

He reached up and touched his wound. "It's clotting. I'm not worried."

Still, she went to the kitchen and fumbled around for rags and water. Returning, she saw he had the computer up and running, and she caught her first glimpse of his face in the light. There was already a bruise forming on the side of his face. She gently wet the rags and wiped the dried blood that had streamed down his cheek into his neck.

"You don't need to do this. I'll take care of it in a moment."

"Shush. You're hurt worse than you're letting on." Her hand paused on his cheek as she took in the swelling. Slowly, her gaze drifted to his eyes. They glittered in the screen light. He really was a very handsome man. It didn't seem fair that the first man who had drawn her attention in a long time turned out to be someone she may have to have fired. When she spoke, her voice sounded clogged. "Sometimes in the moment, we think we're doing what's best for everyone, but we're blinded from pertinent details. I dig for those details so I can make a good choice."

He reached his hand up and covered hers on his cheek. "What details do you need to know that would let you trust me?"

"What did your partner say when you left him on the boat?"

Victor frowned and dropped his gaze away from her. "He asked me not to go. He said there wasn't enough time."

It was the one response she couldn't accept. It meant he was risky out in the field with the other team members. He was just as risky as Shiloh. Quickly, she hurried her movements to finish cleaning his face, then took the bucket and rags to the kitchen. She grabbed a couple of ice packs, and when she returned, he was kneeling gingerly by the fire, stoking it and bringing it to a full flame. When she saw him struggle to get back on his feet, she rushed to his side and let him use her arm to pull himself up.

"Do you think your leg is broken?" she asked.

"It's workable. Perhaps a fracture, but nothing to worry about."

They returned to the couch, agreeing to stay there for the night. "I need to call Tyson and let him know we made it," Victor said, reaching for his phone in his pocket.

"I already sent him a text. When I was in the kitchen," she informed him.

"Did you tell him what I told you about the yacht?"

Jodie sighed and leaned back on the couch, putting her feet up on the ottoman. "I almost did. But, no. Not yet."

"What held you back? He is your boss. You have to tell him what you found."

She turned quickly to face him. "Maybe I still have some hope."

At his raised brow, she could see him trying to figure out what she meant by *hope*. Did she dare tell him? "There is a part of me that wants to see you succeed. I know not everything is black and white. I know newspapers can be skewed and biased. And I know how to read between the lines. I still have hope that what I find between those lines vindicates you. But I also can't wait much longer. Your probation should be ending soon, and Tyson needs another handler. I just have to make sure that you will have the team's back. If any of them tell you they need you to stay, I need to know that you will follow orders."

"I understand. And I appreciate your grace in this matter. I know I don't deserve a second chance." He looked over at the dogs lying by the fire. "I think I understand why you give Shiloh the same. You see something in him worth saving. And I'm honored that you see something in me as well."

Her phone buzzed, and looking down, she could see that it was SAC Bridges. "Hello, sir, how can I help you?" she asked.

"I owe you an apology, Jodie. I messed up." His words caught her off guard.

"What do you mean?" She straightened up on the couch.

"I mean Monica contacted me two weeks ago, and I did not respond. Her message got put by the wayside, and I let her down. She had sent me a letter saying that her company was making an illegal chemical and selling it on the black market. I should've put a team on it, but with the RMKU and my office working urgent cases and the holidays coming up, I put off assigning it until after vacation."

Jodie leaned forward, resting her elbows on her knees. The thought formed in her mind that Monica was dead because Bridges didn't respond to her letter, but the accusation sat on her tongue. She glanced at Victor and took a deep breath, deciding to read between these lines. "Is there anything else?" She needed all the details to make a decision.

"The fire investigators found an explosive at Monica's house. It wasn't a gas leak. She survived that—but by then I'd already let her down. I've put a whole team on it now."

"She was trying to let people know, and it got her killed," Jodie said. She felt Victor touch her shoulder gently and she leaned into it. It felt good to have him beside her during this moment. "This is so sad."

"My family keeps telling me I need a break. Some R and R. I'm supposed to be at the lake house tomorrow night for Christmas Eve. But I don't feel like I deserve it right now."

"Go. Your team is on it. There is nothing else you can do."

"Are you safe right now?" She could hear his desperate tone, as he clearly wanted to make sure he didn't walk away when she needed him.

"For the time being. We're locked up in Daniella's lodge."

"Good. You call if you need anything. And I'm so sorry."

Jodie figured it had to have taken him a lot to make this call. She looked to Victor and said, "I appreciate that. And I appreciate your humility." The phone disconnected, but she kept it at her ear. Slowly, she brought it down to her lap. "And I appreciate yours, Victor. If Bridges can slip up, then anyone can. Everyone deserves another chance to prove themselves." She told herself that she wasn't extending this second chance because of her hidden feelings for Victor. However, the fight within her disagreed. She would be lying if she said her feelings for him wasn't a factor.

He reached for her hand, and this time he entwined her fingers through his. "You are amazing. But I knew that the first moment I laid eyes on you." He smiled, a bit nervously. "You mentioned that you had hope. Well, so did I."

"I figured that when you brought me daisies." The direction of this conversation could lead to discord within the office, but it was a conversation that they needed to have.

He looked sheepish. "I thought they matched your personality." He shrugged. "I'm sorry if it was inappropriate."

"It wasn't inappropriate. I really like them."

"Maybe I'll get you some more someday."

"I still have them." Jodie wondered if revealing that secret was the best choice. At his surprised look, she continued, "I dried them and pressed them in my Bible. I put them in Proverbs three." As she quoted the scripture, she watched his lips move with her voice. He knew it as well. He wasn't just a praying man—he really followed God. It made her question her doubts in him.

"When we trust in God, He will make our paths

straight," Victor said. "And, Jodie, I believe my path has led me…" He leaned closer. "To the RMKU."

For a moment, she thought he was going to say to her, but that wouldn't have been right, would it? "To the RMKU?"

He frowned a bit. "Yeah, and maybe to someone else, too. I'm trying to figure that out still."

With him so close, she dropped her gaze to his lips and felt her resolve toward him melting. When she looked back into his eyes, she could tell he wanted to kiss her. For a moment, she thought maybe one kiss, but shook her head. It wasn't possible. Before she could voice her decision, the sound of a car door shutting alerted them both and made their choice for them.

Victor pulled back, jumped to his feet and let out a slight groan at the pain in doing so. "Stay here. Cleo, come."

Cleo jumped to her feet, but so did Shiloh, sidling up against the yellow Lab.

Jodie pointed to Shiloh. "Sit," she said and signed. "You're not going anywhere until we know you can be trusted." She didn't need Shiloh putting Victor in more danger with his hesitancy.

"Actually, I'll take Shiloh. I want Cleo guarding you."

"But what if he doesn't perform?" Concern threaded her voice. She may be hesitant to trust the man, but she didn't want him dead. That sudden realization caught her off guard. She couldn't deny the fact that she really did care for him.

After he left the lodge, Jodie wrestled with that fact. Thinking the man was attractive and caring about him were two different things. But after more time lapsed, she realized that he had left her, just as he had left the woman on the yacht.

And he had taken her dog.

Standing up, she led Cleo into the kitchen to grab a

knife in the butcher block. She didn't know how to use it, but it felt good just to have some sort of weapon.

Suddenly, Cleo barked and moved in a circle. She was trying to give Jodie a message. Jodie thought about Cleo's experience as an explosives-detecting K-9. She realized Cleo was giving the same sign she had back in the parking garage next to her car.

Jodie swallowed hard as she realized that could only mean one thing.

There was a bomb in the kitchen.

NINE

Victor found the parked car on the side of the lodge. It was still warm from someone driving it in, but there was no one around. The plates on the vehicle were from New Mexico and not Colorado, but that didn't mean it wasn't their killer. He could have easily stolen the vehicle after he rammed his other car into the SUV, especially if the perp's had been damaged to the point that it was undrivable.

He signed and whispered to Shiloh to follow him. The dog stayed by his side, alert and ready. So it wasn't all the time that he hesitated. But all it took was once to get someone killed.

Staying in the shadows of the tree line around the perimeter of the property, he searched for someone who may have been hiding. He kept the view of the front door in his sights just in case their visitor decided to go in that direction. Coming back around, he stopped to listen for any unusual sounds. He heard nothing, but he also knew he wasn't alone. Then, as he turned back to the lodge, a woman's voice spoke out in the darkness…and it wasn't Jodie's.

"Shiloh, come," she said.

Once again, the dog didn't hesitate and raced off into the trees.

Victor removed his sidearm at the same moment he heard the click of the person's weapon in the woods. He couldn't take aim in the dark, but he knew her gun was targeted right on him.

"Who are you?" he asked.

"Since you're on my property, you can answer that question for me. Who are you and why do you have Jodie's dog?" She stepped into the clearing, her gun held at eye level and aimed at him.

"I'm Victor Abrams, and you must be Daniella." He held up his hands, hoping this was the case.

"Where is Jodie?"

He jutted his chin in the direction of the lodge. "She's inside. We kept the lights off for obvious reasons."

Suddenly, Jodie shouted, "Victor! I think there's a bomb! Victor, where are you?" He could hear the distress in her voice.

"I'm off to your left," he responded, his arms still up. "See? I'm on your side. Can you take the gun off me now?"

Jodie turned on a flashlight and bounced it around to find him. The beam took in him, and then Daniella. "Daniella!" Jodie picked up her pace and ran toward her friend. "What are you doing here?"

Daniella did the same, lowering her weapon to take Jodie into her arms for a hug. For a moment the two women held each other. "I may not be an officer at the RMKU anymore, but I still had to be sure you made it here safely."

"We almost didn't. The guy smashed his car into ours and nearly sent us over the cliff."

"And now there's a bomb?"

Jodie stepped out of her embrace and said, "Cleo sensed something in the kitchen. It could be a bomb. She did the same thing with my car and that had a bomb attached."

Victor stepped close to them. "I'm going in with Cleo to check it out." He looked to Daniella. Now in Jodie's flashlight beam, he could see she was a tall, strongly built woman. She wore her jet-black hair to her collar with her forehead revealed. Her tough, no-nonsense demeanor told him Jodie would be fine in her care. Daniella had been a RMKU officer until a few months ago and been replaced by his teammate, Gavin Walker.

"It's nice to meet you," he told her. "Keep her safe."

"Always," Daniella responded with her arm around Jodie's shoulders.

At that, Victor and Cleo headed toward the possible explosive.

"The new handler is cute," Daniella whispered after Victor entered the house.

"Yeah, it's just too bad he has a mark against him. I uncovered something about his past that makes me nervous."

"Did a red flag come up on his security checks?" Daniella asked as she led the way to her car.

"No, Tyson wouldn't have hired him if it had. On paper, Victor Abrams is a stellar match for the RMKU."

"So what's the problem?"

Jodie opened the rear door for Shiloh while her friend opened the passenger door for her. Daniella was five years older than she was, and even though they were good friends, Daniella always felt like an older sister watching out for her.

"He had an incident in the navy that he has been cleared of, but the fact still remains that he did leave his team member…who didn't survive."

Daniella whistled through her teeth. "I'm glad to hear he was absolved of wrongdoing, but the unit needs to trust him with their lives."

"Exactly. And if I have to end up having him fired, it won't matter how I feel about him."

"Feel about him? Is there something I should know?"

Jodie winced, having said too much. "Have I told you

how much I miss you at the unit?" Jodie asked, trying to change the subject.

Before Daniella shut the door, she said, "You're avoiding the question." She closed it and came around the other side, climbing in behind the wheel. "Now, spill."

"I'm serious. I'm so happy for you and Sam, but I miss you and our talks in the office."

Daniella looked at her lodge. "I miss them, too, and you, of course." She looked back at Jodie. "You like him, don't you?"

Jodie nodded once. "I think so. Not that I would ever act on it. The team always comes first."

"Trust your instincts, Jodie. You're amazing at your job. If Victor is a risk to RMKU, you'll know what to do. And if he's an asset, you'll know that, too. I support you with whatever you decide."

Jodie smiled at her friend. "I really do miss you." She leaned close and hugged Daniella. Then her phone buzzed. Jodie pulled back to see Tyson was calling her. She answered quickly. "What's up, boss? Daniella is with me." She put him on speaker.

"Great. We've identified our suspect. He's one of the chemists in the lab that Monica worked at. His name is Liam Bryce, and according to his bank-account records, he's been making a pretty penny selling illegal chemicals on the black market. Way more than his salary."

"As soon as I get on the computer, I'll see what I can find on him, too," Jodie said.

"The guy is on to us investigating him now. None of his associates have seen him or can reach him."

She closed her eyes for a moment and asked, "So now that he knows killing me won't keep him protected, will he back off?" She peered into the darkness, toward the lodge, knowing Victor was inside and putting his life at risk.

"Don't count on it. Now he's backed into a corner.

Bridges has a whole team searching for him. He's contacted New Mexico's FBI office as well."

Daniella said, "It's not safe for her to stay here. And honestly, I want this guy away from the lodge. We've had enough go down here. I don't need any more. Victor and Cleo are inside right now sweeping the place for a possible explosive."

Jodie frowned at her friend. "I'm so sorry for bringing this to your doorstep."

Daniella gave her a warning glare. "Don't you even go there. I told you to come, and I don't regret it. But Tyson is right. This man is going to retaliate even more. He's cornered now and most likely will come out with guns blazing, not caring who gets hurt. Even family. I can't bring that to Sam and Oliver. He found you up on the road, and he's bound to find you here, if he hasn't already."

Tyson said, "Yeah, I'd like her back up here, where I can bring the handlers in to protect her."

"We don't have a working car," Jodie said.

Tyson grumbled through the line. "Do I want to know what happened?"

"We had a run-in with the guy," Jodie admitted.

Daniella frowned. "I'll get her back to Denver, Tyson. Don't worry about her."

"Thanks, Daniella. Keep me informed." Tyson clicked off.

As Jodie held her phone, she noticed the clock on it said that it was midnight. "It's Christmas Eve. But it sure doesn't feel like it. I had plans to go see my mom for dinner. She has no idea why I canceled."

Daniella nodded to the phone. "Call her. You may not get another chance. And you need to give her some directions so she's safe."

The gravity of Daniella's statement had Jodie dialing

her mother's number. After a few rings, her mother's tired face appeared on her screen.

"Hi, Mom," Jodie signed. "I'm sorry to wake you up. I just wanted to say I'm sorry I can't be there for dinner tomorrow."

Suki Chen signed, "We understand. We know you are very busy. I will make you a plate just in case."

Jodie squeezed the tears forming behind her glasses. She didn't want her mom to see her fear that this might be the last time they ever saw each other. "I'd appreciate that. And some pie. You know how much I love your chocolate cream."

"Double portion," Suki signed, and Jodie smiled with a nod.

"Hey, Mom, I need you to do me a favor. Keep your doors locked and keep Harley with you at all times." Her mother's Great Dane wasn't much of an attack dog, but he was big.

Suki's face grew concerned. "Why? Is something wrong? Jodie, what aren't you telling me? Are you hurt?"

"No. No." She didn't want to concern her mom—she just wanted to be sure her mother took some precautions. If Daniella was correct, Liam Bryce might hurt Jodie by going after her family. "I'm good. I'm safe." *For now.* "Just do this for me, okay?"

Suki signed, "Yes. Anything for you."

"Thank you. Goodbye, Mom." Jodie clicked off and took the deepest breath to fill her lungs. "That was so hard."

"I'm so sorry, honey." Daniella reached out for Jodie's shoulder and gave her a squeeze. "You did good. I'm proud of you. You're a tough cookie."

Jodie smiled through tears at her friend. "Not as tough as you."

"I beg to differ." Daniella nodded toward the lodge.

"Victor's on his way back. Stay here," she said, climbing out of the car.

The two met in front of the vehicle, and Victor showed Daniella a small box. They spoke quietly to themselves for a moment, and at Daniella's nod, Victor came around to the passenger side and opened the door to show Jodie.

"Well?" Jodie asked, looking up at him.

He crouched down to her eye level and came very close to her. "Yes, it's a bomb, but it's a dud." He showed her a small box with a ticking digital clock. But the wires were disconnected. "He wasn't going to blow up the lodge with this. He might have planted it just to scare you into running from the lodge."

"Which is exactly what I did." Jodie dropped her forehead into her palm. "If you and Daniella weren't here, I would have run right into his trap."

Jodie lifted her head and looked at the clock and how it was counting down 24 hours to zero. "The timer says that it's going to be at zero at midnight on Christmas morning. Could it be a warning? Or another trap? Or is he trying to tell me that's how long I have to live?"

"Shh." Victor brushed her cheek. "Don't try to make sense of this guy. Don't give him that power."

"How can I not? He's after vengeance now. Because of me, the RMKU and the FBI know who he is. He won't stop until he kills me." She could hear the fear in her own voice and see it mirrored in his blue, piercing eyes.

"I won't let it happen," he said. "Listen to me, I am going to keep you safe. I promise."

Jodie looked to Daniella, who was standing behind the door. "Tyson called and told us his identity." Jodie looked back at Victor and relayed the message fully and what Liam Bryce did at the lab. "We can't stay here."

"No. We're leaving." He glanced behind him. "Daniella's agreed to come with us and drive us back. We need to get back to Denver and find out what this man has planned on Christmas. He could be after any of us now."

Jodie leaned closer. "Victor, with Bryce's access to explosives and chemicals, it could be catastrophic."

Victor cupped her cheek and rubbed beneath her glasses with his thumb. "I know..." She could see in his pained expression that he knew all about catastrophe.

TEN

Victor felt they were playing right in to this man's hands. As Daniella drove her car, Jodie sat in the passenger seat and Victor was in the back with the K-9s, staying in contact with Tyson. Their last phone call ended with Tyson informing him that he would order his team in Denver to be on the lookout. He would have them all inspect their homes and have SAC Bridges do the same thing for his agents, just in case Bryce had planted any explosives on their personal properties.

With eleven hours between Silver City and Denver, that didn't leave him very much time before midnight to figure out what this man's next move would be.

Jodie had the laptop open, and the light from the screen illuminated her face.

"Did you find anything on him?" he asked. She had been pulling searches for the last few hours.

"I've hit some firewalls I'm trying to hack," she said without looking up. "But he definitely has a presence on the black market. Looks like he's been selling for a while. Some cartels and terrorist organizations."

Once again, Victor was impressed by this woman. "Will I have to scrub my computer after this?" He smiled when she looked his way.

She smiled back. "I'll vouch for you if the FBI come knocking. I know some people."

Cleo lifted her head and whined. Shiloh slept soundly on the other side of her.

"It won't be much longer now," he said, patting her. She lowered her head onto his knee and huffed.

Daniella said from behind the wheel, "How long have you had her? She's pretty mild-tempered."

"Yeah, she's been with me for the last six years in the navy. Her main task was underwater explosives. She's got a good sniffer and can detect at least twenty feet below the surface."

"How come she only worked for six years?" Daniella asked.

Victor shifted in the seat, feeling a little uneasy with this conversation. He looked down at his dog and continued to pet her. "She was injured. The navy figured they would retire her when I retired. But she still has a few more years left in her to work on land. I figured the RMKU would be a little less rigorous than the ocean." When he looked up, he saw that Jodie had turned to stare at him.

"How was she injured?" she asked.

"It was the yacht explosion." He hoped that would be the end of the conversation.

"No, *how* was she injured? How was she hurt?"

"You don't have to worry. She can do her job. She has no fear on land." *Except for fire.*

"I'm not worried about her doing the job. I'm worried about *her*. I do have a heart, you know." Jodie held his gaze with an intensity that drilled into him.

"I appreciate your caring, I really do, but I don't want to get into it right now." He looked out the window to nothing but blackness.

"We still have a few hours left to drive." When he didn't respond, Jodie said, "Victor, I won't tell anyone."

He watched Daniella look to her friend quickly, then back to the road. Everything was quiet, and he could tell they both waited for him to speak.

"We got trapped under the flames." He closed his eyes, still seeing the black-and-gold flickering with no opening to get through above him. "She nearly drowned before I found an escape. After that, she grew timid around the water…and around flames. That doesn't bode well for a navy K-9."

"And you? How did you fare?"

He shrugged. "I lost my partner. I have no place to complain."

Jodie turned back around to face the laptop, and they drove on in silence for a while. After a few minutes, Tyson called back.

"We found nothing. Every house is clean. Bryce doesn't seem to be targeting the RMKU or the FBI. How much longer before you arrive?"

Daniella answered, "Two hours."

"Okay, the team will be meeting here soon, so come right to the office. The clock is ticking." Tyson clicked off, and for the rest of the ride, an uneasy feeling surrounded them.

Cleo picked up her head and whined again, obviously sensing the tension. Victor dug his fingers into her fur and let her comfort him, and he did the same for her, as they had since the yacht explosion. He dropped his head to hers and breathed in her sweetness. When he straightened back up, he caught Jodie watching him with a frown. She quickly turned back to her computer, and nothing was said for the rest of the ride.

Jodie led the way into the RMKU office with Daniella behind her and Victor and the dogs following them. She faced the handlers with their own dogs, all in various positions around the main room. Some sat, while some paced in an unnerving silence. A few stood over by the Christmas tree, with its dog ornaments twinkling. She was sure this was not how any of them had envisioned they would be spending Christmas Eve.

Tyson walked up to her with Denver PD officer Skylar Morgan beside him. She reached a slender hand and rubbed Jodie's shoulder. Concern flooded her green eyes as she tilted her long, wavy red hair.

"I'm so sorry this danger is at your doorstep. I'm so thankful you're okay." Skylar would soon marry Tyson. Jodie couldn't be happier for them.

"I'm just glad I didn't miss your wedding," Jodie said, giving her best upbeat response. She didn't want anyone to feel bad for her. Monica was the only victim here.

Tyson took her in his arms and gave her a quick hug. "I'm glad to have my right-hand woman back. But we'll all take it from here. You're to stay out of the line of fire. You hear?" He pulled back and looked down at her.

"No problem, boss. I'm going to stick behind my monitors from now on."

Tyson and Skylar returned to the group, inviting Daniella in. "Thank you for bringing them back. You're welcome to sit in and help us strategize. Perhaps you'll see something we're missing. We searched everyone's homes and headquarters. Jodie could be the sole target, but any of us could be, too. And with only eight hours remaining, we're all a little wound up."

Victor brought Jodie a chair, and she took it, sitting beside him with the group. She instructed Shiloh and Cleo to sit with her sign commands. The K-9s settled at their feet right away.

One of the handlers brought in from his Christmas vacation was Ben Sawyer. He sat across from her with his wide brown eyes on Shiloh. "I'm impressed, Jodie. Perhaps Shiloh deserves a second chance if he can follow your signs so obediently." The perpetual black-haired scruff on his cheeks and chin creased with a smile.

She shrugged. "He seems to follow Cleo. I wouldn't say it's perfect yet. Maybe you've all been right and I shouldn't be investing time into him. But I'm just not ready to give up yet."

Victor said, "Her ability to give second chances is astounding. And humbling." He said the last part under his breath for only her to hear.

She had a decision to make. Jodie thought back to the moment she watched Victor drop his head to Cleo's in the car. She had been so worried about him leaving the team behind, she neglected to see that not only had he been trapped and faced his own death, but he really hadn't left his partner behind in that yacht fire. When it came down to Cleo's safety, Victor stayed right beside her and got her out of the flames, even at the expense of his own life. And when the navy thought Cleo needed to be retired, Victor went with her.

In that moment, Jodie made the decision that some newspaper reporter's opinion on the Mariana Islands did not have the power or authority to cancel out Victor's already stellar record.

"I want Victor to be put on the case," she announced. "His probationary period has been long enough. He brings a lot to the team and shouldn't sit this out."

Victor stood up abruptly. "Wait." He looked down at her. "You don't have to do this. I want everything on the table." He turned and scanned the room. "What Jodie's not telling you is that in my last mission, I left my partner on the boat to try and defuse the bomb beneath. He asked me not to go, and I went, anyway."

Tyson took a step forward, concern growing on his face. "And what happened to him?"

Victor held his head high but swallowed hard. "Neither him nor the woman we were rescuing made it out alive. By the time I located the bomb, it was too late. Perhaps, if I had stayed aboard, I could have…" He trailed off on a sigh that tugged at Jodie's heart.

She had to say something. If she didn't, he might never stop blaming himself. "But what he's not telling you is that he was trapped by flames on the water. And that he never left Cleo's side. He got her to safety and out of the fire. That has to count for something. Please don't hold this against him. Give him a chance to prove himself."

She watched many of the faces drop to look down into their laps. For a few moments, no one said anything, and she knew they needed to process their responses.

Suddenly, the door burst open and SAC Bridges stormed in. "I know where the bomb is." The man's typical calm countenance had disappeared. His hair was disheveled, his suit coat wrinkled and his collar open. Jodie had never seen him look like this.

Tyson stepped up to him. "Well? We need direction. Time is running out."

Bridges's face nearly crumpled. "Liam Bryce called me. The bomb is at my family's lake house on Lake Riviera." His lips trembled. "My whole family is there. They're expecting me for dinner. I've tried to reach them over and over, but no one is answering. I've sent my agents out there, but I would like all your help as well." He looked around the room, pleading for their acceptance.

One by one each person stood up and committed to going.

Tyson moved right into issuing orders. He went around the room, and as he did, the handlers and their dogs left for their assigned tasks. When he reached Jodie and Victor, he paused.

Jodie stood up beside Victor, waiting for Tyson's decision.

After some hesitancy, he shook his head. "I can't allow it. I can have no regrets. I'm sorry. Remain here with Jodie and Daniella. We'll discuss your future with the RMKU later." With that, he turned his back on Victor and went to join his team. Long after they were gone, Victor still hadn't said a word.

Jodie looped her arm through his, trying to get his attention. Slowly, he turned her way, startled to see she was still standing beside him.

"You didn't have to do that," she said.

"Yes, I did. I should have done it on day one. There can be no secrets within the team. We're only as strong as our weakest link, and they were right to leave me out. And you would be smart to do the same." He stepped away, signaling his dog to come, and headed to his desk.

Jodie turned to find Daniella standing in the doorway to her office. Jodie walked up to her, and as she passed her, Daniella whispered, "It's too bad. I really liked him."

Jodie whispered sadly, "Me, too."

ELEVEN

Jodie hung up with Tyson after listening to his discouraging update and knew what she had to do, whether her boss liked it or not. She left her office for the bullpen and came around the side of Victor's cubicle. He had his back to her and appeared to be reading something. To his right she noticed a box of belongings on his desk already packed to go. On the top was a collection of books. One was on sign language. Her heart twisted at the sight.

She always thought she was a good researcher, but she'd failed to remember that it was the personal details of a person that painted the most accurate picture.

"Victor? Can I talk to you?" she asked quietly, not wanting to startle him.

He turned quickly, and she saw that he was reading his Bible. Once again, this man surprised her. "Absolutely." He stood to give her his chair. He went to the adjacent cubicle to grab a chair for himself. Sitting in it, he leaned forward with expectant eyes. "Go ahead, Jodie. Don't worry about hurting me. I can take it."

"Hurting?" She looked to the opened Bible, splayed to the Book of Proverbs. "I didn't come here to hurt you." She looked back at him. "The team needs you. Tyson just called and Bridges's family is not there. There's no sign of any explosives at the lake house. It appears to have been a trick. And now there's only four hours left, and his family is missing."

Victor leaned back as he processed this information. "And he wants me to come?"

She looked down at her hands in her lap and shook her head. "But I think you should."

She felt the tip of his finger under her chin, lifting her face to his. "That would be against orders. I want to prove that I can follow them. I know Tyson said that he would have to discuss my future here, but I also know God brought me here. My path has led me to the RMKU and to…"

She knew what he was about to say.

To her.

He dropped his hand to his knee. "Never mind."

Slowly, Jodie reached across and covered his hand. Gripping it tight, she said, "Tyson only said that because he doesn't know you. He doesn't see what I see. You belong with the team. I'll go with you. With time running out, they need all hands on deck."

Victor tilted his head while his brow furrowed in thought. "The reason I ran out of time on the Mariana Islands is because our victim wasn't where we were told she would be. By the time we figured out that she was on the yacht, it was too late. Jodie—" He leaned forward again, his eyes darkening with intensity. "Did Tyson say if they searched the water for his family? Are there any boats still on the lake?"

"No, he didn't say. See? This is why you need to be there. You and Cleo have experience that could be beneficial. Daniella said we can take her car. She's sleeping in my office. She needs to rest before she drives back to her family in the morning. What do you say? If Tyson gets mad, I will speak up for you. I will take the blame."

A slow smile spread across his face, and his blue eyes

glimmered. "I've never had a champion before. I sure could have used you this past year." He turned his hand and entwined his fingers through hers. "Thank you, Jodie." He breathed deep and stood, pulling her up with him. "I'll get the dogs."

Having their minds made up, they led the K-9s out to the parking garage and into Daniella's car. Jodie drove to Lake Riviera, and the weight of the pending doom had them deep in their own thoughts the whole way.

The body of water wasn't that big at only seventeen acres, and as she drove around it, Victor studied its surface beyond the homes built on the waterfront.

"From what I can see the few boats out there are winterized. They seem to all be wrapped, but Bryce wouldn't put a flag on one if he's planning on blowing it up."

Along with Bridges's family. Jodie kept her thought to herself. She drove around the lake and came to the lake house. The team's cars were parked in the street, along with FBI vehicles. She parked the car and headed inside with Victor and the dogs.

As soon as they entered, Tyson stepped forward in obvious irritation.

Jodie held up her hand. "He's here because I asked him to be. He has experience in explosives. I think you need to hear him out. You would be foolish not to. You hired him, Tyson, for a reason. Remember that reason and give him a chance."

Skylar stepped up beside Tyson and touched his arm. She offered him a look that seemed to work as the sergeant relented and waved for Victor to enter. "If you have any ideas, we'd love to hear them."

Victor faced the group and asked, "Have you searched the boats?"

SAC Bridges replied, "Our boat is stored for the winter. It's not here."

"We just drove the perimeter of the lake, and there are some boats out there. They're winterized and wrapped, but to me, that makes them a prime location for an explosive to go undetected. It's why we didn't detect the bomb in the Mariana Islands. We were looking on land, and the water kept the dogs from detecting any explosives. Until I took her into the water off the yacht." He reached down and patted Cleo's head. "I'd like to take her out and see if she detects anything. The closer we get, she'll pick up a scent." He looked to Bridges. "What do you have for underwater gear?"

"I have a wetsuit and an oxygen tank with a regulator. You're free to use them, but I'm sure I don't have to tell you that water is freezing."

"I'm aware of that. Do you have a kayak I can row out in?"

"I'll go grab it down from the rafters. And I'll arrange for more suits for my agents just in case they all need to head out in that water."

RMKU K-9 handler Nelson Rivers said, "I can call Mia. She can get us all the equipment we need." Mia Turner used to own an outdoor supply shop and knew whom to call. Nelson had also been called off one of his own cases to help beat the clock tonight. He would soon marry Mia... if any of them made it out of here alive tonight.

"Great." With that, Bridges left the room, leaving everyone planning their next move if Victor was right.

Tyson ordered a helicopter, but Victor stopped him. "Alerting Bryce that we might be on to him could make him speed things up."

Tyson asked, "Is that what happened to you?"

At Victor's nod, Jodie frowned. There was so much more to the story than that article stated. If Victor had thought that he had more time to get the woman off the yacht, then leaving his partner wouldn't have seemed that much of a risk.

Tyson pressed his lips into a tight line. "Okay, we will hold off until you give us the go-ahead. We just hope that this last-ditch effort will lead us down the right path. I don't even want to imagine the devastation if we don't find this device in time. Families have already tucked their children into their beds for Christmas morning." The solemn thought quieted the room. They had to find this bomb in time. "Everyone else, break up into different locations in case Bryce sets a trap to get rid of us all. Stand by for orders."

Victor turned and captured Jodie's attention. The look of admiration in his eyes pulled on her heartstrings. She knew without a doubt that he was right where he was supposed to be, that God had led him right to this moment for redemption. She lifted her hands and signed as she said, "God, lead Victor and be with him down every path and carry him to the end."

As everyone said, "Amen," he lifted his hand to his lips and signed to her, "Thank you, Jodie."

Victor stepped out from the garage with a wetsuit on. He had put a child's suit on Cleo. Bridges's lake-house garage had assorted wetsuits for all the family members of every age.

"Is that going to be enough for her?" Jodie asked from the front steps. He hadn't realized she was waiting for him, and her presence startled him.

"You should be inside. It's cold out here," he said. "And the gear is better than nothing. There's not enough time to bring in anything else."

"I'll be sure to order her own gear for the future."

"That would be really sweet of you."

"Nothing sweet about it. You can't do your job if you

don't have the right equipment. And that includes our K-9 officers as well." She stepped down off the steps and came closer. The two lanterns on the side of the garage illuminated her as she stepped into his space. He kept his hands at his side to keep from reaching for her.

"Well, I hope that Cleo and I get to stay on at the RMKU." His voice thickened.

"Victor," she said softly. "I want you to be careful out there."

"Always."

She took another step closer, placing her hand on his chest. "I can feel your heart racing. I know you're scared. You don't have to pretend with me."

He reached up and covered her hand with his. Lying to her didn't feel right. "The fear will keep me focused. I have to protect Cleo. And as for my heart, it always does when you're near."

In this moment, truth was all that mattered. The possibility of never seeing her again was real. He knew all too well how fast the device could blow. There was also the possibility that the timer that Bryce left them was a trick. Victor knew that even if he found the explosive, it could go off at any time.

"I want to thank you for what you did inside, with the team. No one has ever done something like that for me," he admitted.

She took another step closer and lifted her face to him, now mere inches away. "I'm sorry I waited so long. If I could go back—"

"No, no regrets. You had a job to do, and that is honorable. We only go forward from here." The fact that they might not have a future hung between them. As the seconds ticked down to a midnight explosion, they knew they could also have mere moments to speak from their hearts.

And yet, words wouldn't do.

He could hear the blood rushing in his head as he reached behind hers and pulled her toward him. He lowered his lips to hers and let the taste of her sweetness soothe his nerves and fill him with hope—hope that this wouldn't be all they ever had.

She turned her head and melted into him as her arms reached around his neck. She broke their connection and put her head on his shoulder as she held him tight. He wrapped his arms tighter around her and did the same. If only he could stay there all night, holding her. But that was not to be.

"It's time," he said close to her ear.

They relaxed their arms around each other, but he held her hand as they walked around the house and down to the dock. Tyson, Skylar and SAC Bridges waited for him with a kayak.

"There's a small oxygen tank for you and a handheld one for Cleo," Bridges said, referencing the tanks in the kayak.

Victor gave Jodie's hand one last squeeze and walked away from her to climb inside with Cleo. He felt his dog's muscles ripple as she sat in the kayak in front of him. "You're doing fine," he said soothingly to her. He could only hope that the trauma of the last time in the water had eased for her. "I need you, girl, to find the device. Do what you do best."

He pushed off from SAC Bridges's dock as the man stood beside Tyson with Skylar and Jodie behind them. The rest of the team had dispersed into groups off the premises. With Bryce demanding the investigation on him be stopped, the man could attempt to take out the whole team at once. If he was desperate enough, he just might try.

As Victor paddled away from shore, he could see every breath he took in the cold night air. The water hadn't frozen yet, but he knew his time under it had to be quick. He was wearing a wetsuit, but it wasn't thick enough for winter. It would bide him some time and was better than nothing, but it wasn't ideal for the frigid conditions.

He paddled in the dark as not to bring any attention to himself, and as he approached the first boat, he pulled up close to it and watched Cleo for any response. Victor was quiet and listened carefully for any people aboard. When Cleo didn't make any motions, he continued on to check another boat. There were only a handful, from what he could see, and after the third boat he was beginning to think he was wrong.

Then he saw a boat in the middle of the water, drifting, and knew he had his boat.

Leaning down, he whispered to Cleo, "Find."

Slowly, he lowered her into the water, slipping in behind her with barely a sound. Once again, Cleo swam beside him, willing to go into the danger, driven to perform a job for the greater good. He had no doubts in her capabilities, but he worried her past trauma would inhibit her in being successful. The temperature also concerned him. He needed to pay attention to how long they would be submerged.

Not wanting to say a word, Victor lifted his hand and gave the sign for Cleo to hunt. She swam slowly and stealthily as she approached the drifting boat. It still had its winter wrap, but as they neared it and circled around, Victor saw that it had been sliced. The Bridges family would be aboard and probably gagged to remain silent. Was Bryce on the boat as well? Victor had to believe that was the case if people weren't calling for help. He held out hope that Bryce wouldn't blow himself up, but that wasn't always the case. Many bombers were willing to give their life for their cause. Either way, Victor couldn't bring attention to himself or Cleo. If she couldn't locate a device outside, Victor would have to board. He could only hope that he would take Bryce by surprise.

The boat extended about twenty feet from bow to stern and appeared to have a room below. If there were windows, the wrap was covering them. Victor and Cleo approached the side and moved slowly around until finally Cleo alerted him that she'd picked up a scent. He put his hand on her head in thanks as he listened for any sounds coming from aboard.

He heard nothing for so long. Then a whimper from either a woman or child. In the next second, the sound of someone slapping another person echoed through the night. Michael's family was definitely onboard, and they were being held captive. This also meant Bryce was on there, which made rescuing Michael's family more difficult. The best way would be to find this device and diffuse it. Victor could only hope he had the time to accomplish this before it detonated. He would have loved to climb aboard and remove them first, just as he should have done with the woman in the Mariana Islands. Once again, he found himself having to make this decision. Knowing the rest of the team waited in the wings to descend on the boat helped him make peace with going after the bomb first.

He checked his watch to see that he had a little less than an hour before midnight. Before he had left the lake house, he had started the countdown until midnight, and as he watched the numbers tick down, he mentally prepared himself for submerging. The last time he had left the surface of the water to search for an explosive had ended tragically.

"Please, God, I ask You to meet me down below." With that, he motioned for Cleo to get low, and she dropped below the surface with only her snout visible. She was doing so well. Better than he could have ever expected her.

Victor brought his mask down from the top of his head and inserted the regulator into his mouth. It was a small tank, so he didn't have long. Probably less than the time left on his watch. Sinking below the surface, he turned his watch's small light on and began to search.

Up and down the hull of the boat, he looked for something that would resemble a device. Cleo had picked up a scent, so he knew it had to be around here. But he also knew she could pick up a scent twenty feet above the device, or to the left or right.

He trailed his hand along the side to feel in the darkness. He dropped lower and found nothing. He went to the left and he could feel nothing but the hull. Swimming back to the right, his hand finally touched a protruding object. Bringing his light back, he could see a small box had been stuck to the side. At the sight, he realized what type of device it was, and he jerked back.

Suddenly, Victor knew what Monica Malone had been signing to Jodie.

RDD.

Radiological dispersal device, also known as a type of dirty bomb with radioactive and illegal material. Just touching it would contaminate him. Which, he just did… and would have to do again to defuse it.

TWELVE

Jodie sat by herself in the lake-house living room as time ticked by. She glanced up at the clock and saw there were thirty minutes left until midnight. Never had she wanted Christmas not to come. She sat in the darkness with only the Christmas tree lights glowing and prayed for Victor's safety. Suddenly, the front door opened, and Nelson and Mia stepped in, with Harlow and Wes.

Jodie stood to welcome them in quickly. "I thought you were all staying separate right now."

Nelson went to the windows to make sure the blinds were all closed securely. "Mia brought in wetsuits and kayaks for everyone, just in case we need them."

Jodie went to Mia and hugged her, thankful that she was able to help secure outdoor equipment. "I appreciate that, but it is dangerous here."

Mia hugged her back. "I understand. But I wanted to be with Nelson tonight."

Jodie could understand that need. So much was up in the air, and anything could happen. She looked to Harlow and Wes. The two of them were expected to be here as a K-9 officer and an FBI agent, but Jodie noticed how the two of them also stuck closer together. As the clock ticked down to midnight, everyone knew that these could be their last moments together. Jodie would love to have been standing beside Victor as well.

She retook her seat and wondered if it was because of the stressful situation and the sense of pending doom. Would she feel the same way if this was just any other ordinary Christmas?

Nelson came and sat beside her. "We need to talk if Victor is going to be staying on. We have a say in this."

"Do we have to talk about this right now?" Jodie asked. "Right now, getting him back safely is all that matters."

"That's fine, but once he is back, we need to be sure that we can trust him. We need to know if he puts the unit first."

"He's out there right now putting his life at risk." Jodie waved toward the lake. "What else would you like him to do?" Nelson always had a hard time trusting anyone, but there was nothing she could say to make him trust Victor. That would have to happen over time as Victor proved himself. "I can attest that he puts his dog before himself. Doesn't that speak for itself?"

Harlow nodded. "I can respect that." She leaned into Wes—obviously the two of them were each other's anchors, and once again, Jodie longed to lean into Victor's strength.

She wondered when he had become so important to her. She had worked hard to avoid her feelings for him and put the job first. Even still, he breached the walls of her heart as easily as she hacked firewalls.

The front door opened, and Bridges and Tyson walked in. They were saying how the FBI agents were quietly evacuating people out of their homes and they were now making plans to head out on the water.

Jodie stood to meet them. "But Victor's not back yet."

Tyson replied, "We can't wait any longer." He looked at everyone in the room. "Gear up. Be down on the water in five minutes."

As Jodie watched everyone disperse, she feared that if they all descended on the boat, they would put Victor in harm's way.

She wondered how that made them any different than him leaving his partner.

She faced Tyson. "I'm going, too."

"You're staying here, and I don't want to hear another word about it." He turned to walk out of the house.

"Fine," she called to his back. "But whatever you do, don't put Victor in jeopardy all because of a newspaper article of one person's opinion about him. Let him prove himself."

She could only hope and pray that Tyson had heard her and would listen.

Victor had no choice but to defuse the bomb. He had removed his wetsuit, and after disconnecting it, he wrapped the device up in his suit. He needed to get it out of the water, knowing it could still leak radioactive materials into the water. But at least, it wouldn't blow tonight.

The devastating aftermath of a radioactive bomb could have taken out miles of human life with the potential of killing long into the future. He had one chance to make sure that never happened. On this night, just moments before Christmas morning, when people had nestled their children into bed and read them stories of joy and hope for the morning to come, they had no idea that Victor Abrams had just risked his own life to give them that.

Victor pushed back from the boat with the device and looked up to where Cleo was swimming, quietly waiting for him to return. Instead, he ascended ten feet away from her. He needed to get her out of the frigid water and back into the kayak, but he had to make sure he didn't touch her. He had enough radioactivity coursing through his body to light up like a Christmas tree.

Breaking through the surface, he motioned for Cleo to follow him, and thankfully she did without a sound. He thought back to the last time he swam with her away from the burning yacht, swimming to a place of safety to save their lives, praying that his partner had rescued the woman in time. Now, there would be no swimming away from the danger, as he now carried it within him.

Checking his watch, he saw it was now Christmas. He figured Liam Bryce would realize something had gone wrong, and as Victor approached his waiting kayak, he could see the man rowing away from the boat toward shore. Had the man planned to blow himself up with the bomb? Everything in Victor wanted to go after him, but to do so would kill the man. He had to hope that the rest of the team and agents on shore would catch him. For now, Victor could only worry about getting Cleo to shore.

When he reached his kayak, he tilted it from one side for her to climb aboard. She jumped in without him having to touch her. He remained in the water as he pulled her to shore. He knew he had been submerged for too long and could feel hypothermia setting in, especially without his wetsuit on. His body trembled and began to grow sluggish. He wondered how long it would be for the radioactive material to shut him down completely, or what would kill him first, the freezing water or contamination. Part of him considered remaining in the water to let hypothermia finish him off quick.

But a certain beautiful young lady waited for him on shore, and he just had to see her one last time.

The light of Bridges's lake house pulled him to shore, one stroke at a time. When he had the kayak close enough that he could push it the rest of the way, he went behind it and used the last bit of his strength to send Cleo forward. He called out the command to go, and she jumped out and on the dock.

Suddenly, he saw Jodie come running down the dock, her feet hitting the wood with quick footsteps.

"Why are you in the water still? You're going to freeze to death." She put her hands over the side to reach for him and help him up.

He swam back. "Don't get close to me. I'm contaminated."

She straightened and tilted her head. "What do you mean?"

"The bomb's been defused. But, Jodie, it was radioactive. Monica was telling you Bryce was selling RDD bombs. Radiological dispersal devices. Dirty bombs that could kill and harm people for miles and for years."

"Oh, Victor. And you touched it?" He could hear her voice catch in the night.

"I had no choice. It was the only way to save many lives."

Jodie slowly came down the dock and sat on the edge. "I don't know what to say. Victor, you could die."

"I know." He wished he could get closer to her, to hold her one last time. But he wouldn't risk her life. "I don't regret anything. Coming here, being part of this team, defusing the bomb, none of it. But especially, I do not regret coming here because of you. I know my path led me straight to you."

He could tell she was crying as he let the water mix with his own tears.

From the shore, he heard the sound of someone clearing their throat, followed by Tyson speaking. "Thank you, Victor. You went above and beyond what I expected, and I apologize for selling you short."

"Not a problem, boss. Tell Bridges he can get his family. It's safe now. And I believe Bryce is on shore somewhere. I saw him rowing away. He's probably not too happy right now to see his efforts thwarted. Can you get Cleo inside and warmed up? She was in the water too long."

"Already taken care of. And if the man is running, the helicopter will spot him. We'll get him. I'm calling an ambulance to see if we can get you into a radioactive wash chamber right away."

"I appreciate that." His voice trembled as his body shook from the cold. He hoped there was a chamber close by. "I have the explosive wrapped in my wetsuit. I'll leave it on the dock. It will need to be disposed of properly."

"I'll take care of it. Don't worry." Tyson gave orders to the team, and Victor watched them file out on the water with their own kayaks and an inflatable raft for the hostages. He gave them directions of how far out it was, and said he heard sounds coming from the boat. He could only hope the Bridges family were all still alive.

"I want you out of the water," Jodie said. She stood from the dock and walked back to shore. "I'm going to put towels and blankets down here. Come out and dry up."

Victor made his way until his feet could touch the ground. He glanced up to see her standing by the blankets. "I need you to back away."

She hesitated, and he understood. "I just want to hold you," she said.

"I know the feeling." He forced a smile. "But, please, I don't want to contaminate you. Can I get a rain check, though?" A man could hope.

Jodie nodded as she stepped away from the blankets and into the shadows, where the lamplight didn't shine. In the next second, she screamed as her feet lifted off the ground and swung out.

Victor ran from the water and halted at the blankets. He could see Liam Bryce choking Jodie from behind. The man wore an air-purified respiratory protective mask. So that's how he planned to protect himself while he killed thousands. "Put her down!" His order fell flat, knowing he could do nothing to help her. To rush in to save her from Bryce's chokehold could end up killing her with radiation instead.

Once again, Victor had a choice to make—to rush in or stay back.

God, make my paths straight and lead me in the way I should go.

Suddenly, Victor saw another movement in the shadows, and he recognized one of the K-9s. It was Shiloh, off to the side, waiting for orders. But Victor didn't want to bring Bryce's attention to him. He also hoped Shiloh would not need coaxing, because he needed Shiloh to save Jodie.

Very carefully, and without uttering a word, Victor made the sign command for Shiloh to guard. In the next second, Shiloh raced forward and leaped into the air, sinking his teeth into Bryce's back and pulling the man down to the ground.

As Bryce's hold on Jodie released, she fell sideways, reaching for her neck.

Victor yelled for help, and a few moments later two FBI agents raced around the house. They descended on Bryce and took over for Shiloh, successfully arresting the corrupt chemist.

"You're under arrest for the murder of Monica Malone and the attempted murder of Jodie Chen, as well as a whole slew of other charges, kidnapping and illegal bomb making and selling just to name a few." The FBI man led Bryce around the house and Victor fell to his knees on the ground. His only focus was Jodie's well-being.

"Did he hurt you?"

She was still holding her neck. "I'll be okay. It's nothing compared to what you have to go through." She turned and reached for Shiloh, signing for the dog to come to her. "Good boy." Jodie dropped her head to the dog and wrapped her arms around his neck. "I always knew you had it in you. I'm so proud of you, and I'm so happy I believed in you."

Victor smiled. "I so wish I could join you two. I'm so happy you believed in him, too. And that you believed in me as well."

She lifted her head from Shiloh's. "And I'm not going to stop believing. However long it takes, I'll be waiting for you, Victor. Whether you like it or not, you're stuck with me."

"Like it? It's the best Christmas present I could ever ask for." Victor knew how certain radiation destroyed a person from the inside out. It was a horrid way to die, and he would never want Jodie to witness it. But for now, as they waited for the ambulance to take him away, he wrapped himself in the blanket and enjoyed these few moments with her on this early Christmas morning.

"When you get out of the hospital, I want to celebrate Christmas with you," she said.

He smiled but made no promises. "I'm thankful to be with you right now. Merry Christmas, Jodie. May all your dreams come true."

The paramedics came around the house, dressed in protective gear and carrying a stretcher. "Victor? We're here to help you."

"The only dream I want to come true is for this to be all over with," Jodie said as the paramedics lowered the stretcher beside him. "And I won't stop dreaming it until you're home."

Victor climbed on and turned his face toward her. "I love you, Jodie." She sat beside her dog, her arm still around him, and he fused the image to his mind, never wanting to forget her sweet nature and beauty.

"I love you, too."

With that, the paramedics took him away, and he could hear her soft cries muffled in her dog's fur.

THIRTEEN

"Any word on Victor?" Tyson asked Jodie as the sun came up on Christmas morning. She sat on her couch in her office with Daniella beside her and hadn't slept at all since the paramedics took him away.

Shaking her head, she said, "I don't know if the hospital will call us. All I want to do is go there and stay beside him."

Tyson led his K-9 to the mat, where Cleo and Shiloh were snuggled together after a long night. He pulled up a chair and sat across from her, leaning forward with his hands folded.

"They'll call me, but they won't let you in. The best thing you can do is get some sleep." He looked at Daniella. "Are you heading back today?"

"I am. I just want to make sure Jodie's okay before I leave."

Jodie knew she looked a mess. "Believe it or not, I'm okay. No news is good news."

Tyson cleared his throat. "And what if it's not good news?"

She fought against the frown tugging at her lips as Daniella took her hand. "I will be brave for him, whatever the diagnosis." She knew the outcome of Victor's health and life depended on the kind of radioactive material the bomb had in it. The fact that Monica was killed for alerting the FBI about Liam Bryce making this material there was a chance the doctors wouldn't even know how to treat him.

A knock came on her door, and Skylar stepped in with Jodie's mom. "Someone's here to see you," Skylar announced, stepping out of the way for Suki Chen to hold her arms out to her daughter.

Jodie jumped from her seat and ran right into her mother's embrace. Her mom rubbed her back and comforted her like only a mother could.

When Jodie stepped back, her mother signed, "You love him?" Her soft eyes saw right into Jodie, and there was no denying it. Not that she wanted to.

Jodie signed, "Very much. But I'm scared. What if…?"

Her mom covered her hand and shook her head. "We pray," she signed, and the two of them signed the simple prayer her mother had taught her as a child.

"God, be with us down every path and carry us to the end." Then Suki Chen added, "And carry Victor back to Jodie, healthy and strong and into the future."

Just having her mother there eased her mind and the tension she'd felt.

Then Suki announced that she'd brought food for everyone, and heads began to pop up from behind their cubicles.

"Did someone say food?" Ben asked.

Jodie hadn't realized everyone was still there. "Why haven't you all gone home? It's over. Bryce is in custody. The bomb has been defused. The Bridges family is safe. Go home and have Christmas with your families."

One by one, they stood from their chairs and came out toward her office.

Nelson said, "You are our family and so is Victor. We're waiting to hear from the hospital just like you are."

Jodie felt her eyes well up. She looked to Tyson for confirmation.

"Victor's job is secure, and his probation period has come to an end. Now we just need to make sure he's well."

Wes announced, "But if we can eat right now that would be good, too."

Everybody laughed and Suki went about unloading the packages with her premade meals. As everyone grabbed plates and chairs, they sat around together.

Tyson stood. "I'd like to say grace. I believe we have much to be thankful for this Christmas."

At everyone's nod, they bowed their heads as the head of the Rocky Mountain K-9 Unit opened with a prayer of thanks for their food and the family gathered around. Before he closed his prayer, he said, "And bring our brother home safe and sound."

As everyone voiced their approval and closed with a hearty "amen," Tyson's phone rang. The room went silent as he removed it from his pocket. Jodie passed her plate over to Daniella, and slowly stood up, approaching on the third ring.

"It's the hospital." Tyson glanced from the screen. "Do you want to answer it?" he asked Jodie.

She shook her head and raised her hand. "Can you, please?" In all her previous bravado about standing by Victor, she just didn't think she could handle a bad report at that moment.

Tyson answered it. "Tyson Wilkes." He nodded twice and said, "I see." He listened again intently, then said, "I'll relay the message, thank you."

As he clicked off, the room had never sounded so still. Even the dogs' snores ceased.

"Well?" Jodie asked. "Was that Victor?"

"That was the doctor. After Victor's wash, the doctor started him on iodine treatments and has tested his radiation levels. He wants to keep Victor for another night, but right now his chemical readings look good. The doctor believes being underwater reduced the level of contamination while Victor handled the device. He also doesn't think Victor has anything to worry about down the line. He thinks it's safe to say he has a clean bill of health."

The room erupted into loud cheers as Daniella patted her friend's back and Suki Chen hugged her daughter. The rest of the team came over and lined up to do the same. After, Tyson remained where he was, holding the phone.

"There was more to the message." Everyone quieted down to hear what he had to say. "The doctor said it's Christmas and Victor should spend it with his family. He's given us permission to visit." He looked around the room. "Shall we pick this party up and move it to the hospital?"

Everyone shouted, "Yes." They raced off to pack the food up, leaving Tyson and Jodie alone.

As Jodie processed the good news, she looked up at her boss and said, "I should tell you now that if there's some kind of office rule that frowns upon office relationships, I'm going to break it."

Tyson cracked a smile. "I'll let it slide this once." He wrapped an arm around her shoulders and pulled her in for a hug. "I'm happy for you both. And I'm so happy you are safe. Now let's go bring Christmas to Victor."

With the three dogs in tow, they headed out. Daniella sidled up to Jodie, and they linked arms. On the other side of Denver, Victor waited for her. "Can we stop at the store real fast?" Jodie asked. "I have to pick something up."

Daniella eyed her. "A Christmas gift? I'm sure you will be the only Christmas gift Victor wants."

Jodie felt herself blush, but she had to agree. "Victor's the best gift I could ask for, too. But I still need to stop at the store."

As far as Christmas mornings went, Victor had had better. The hospital seemed exceptionally quiet with a mini-

mal staff bustling around. He'd been isolated all night, but
the doctors were pleased that his radiation readings had
lessened this morning. Still, Victor worried about his future. The chemicals that Liam Bryce used in the device
were meant for mass destruction. For this reason, he hesitated leaving the room, not wanting to make contact with
anyone. But staying in this bed forever wasn't an option.

"It's time for your medication." A nurse entered the
room with a cart. He noticed she did not have the protective gear over her face.

"Please, stay back. I don't want to hurt anyone."

She paused and looked at his chart. "Your readings are
coming down. You've been through the chemical wash.
You're not contaminated anymore."

"But am I safe?"

"As safe as anyone else who comes in these doors." She
put his pills in a paper cup and poured water into a plastic cup. She stepped up beside him to hand them to him.

Instinctively, Victor shrugged back. He looked up at
her. "Are you sure?"

"Mr. Abrams, I wouldn't be here if I wasn't. Now take
your pills." She passed them over to him and he threw
them to the back of his throat and swallowed with the
water. "Good. It's important that you take them to protect
your thyroid."

"Because I still have radiation in me, correct?"

"You're not in the clear yet. But you can enjoy your life
and not worry about hurting others."

"At least not physically." He looked to the wall, where
a television hung in the corner.

The nurse studied him with pursed lips. "Am I correct in
thinking that you're worried about hurting someone down
the road if an illness should transpire from the radiation?"

He nodded once and glanced back at the older woman.
She had gray at her temples and had probably seen a lot

in her years at the hospital. "You probably think I'm being ridiculous, but the not knowing what's to come has me a bit hesitant to walk out of here and go back to my life as if nothing is wrong."

Just then, the most beautiful woman in the world stepped up to the doorway and took his breath away.

Jodie was standing before him.

She smiled so serenely, and behind her glasses, he could see love directed toward him. She was a dream come true, and more than anything, he would have loved to grow old with her. That's what she deserved. Someone to grow old with.

"You shouldn't have come," he said flatly.

The smile on her face fell as she took a step into the room.

"No." He put his hand up. "I don't want to hurt you."

The nurse stepped back to leave the room, but before she exited, she paused beside Jodie and whispered something to her.

Jodie's gaze never left him, and after the nurse left, she continued the rest of the way into the room. Stepping up beside his bed, she reached for his hand.

He pulled it away before she made contact.

"It's too soon," he said. "Please step back. For your own safety."

"I'm not going anywhere, Victor. Get used to it. I don't veer from the path that God has me on. If I trust Him enough to pray for His guidance, then I must trust Him enough to go where He leads." She reached for his hand again, this time taking hold of it.

Victor closed his eyes and silently prayed that he had nothing on him that would hurt her.

Slowly, she turned his hand over and traced along his fingers and over the places where he had held that device and all its destructive materials.

"The chemicals Bryce used were highly potent. It could be years before they manifest some illness in me. Or it could happen next week."

As she held him, she said, "You are the bravest man I've ever met. You saved countless lives last night without a thought to your own. You sit here and continue to want to save more people, including me, but you don't have to do this alone." She stopped tracing on his hand. "Unless, that's what you want."

"No," he said quickly, reaching for her and coming within an inch of her arm. His hand hovered without making contact. "I would never forgive myself if I hurt you."

She looked to his hand and back to him. "Then let me make that decision." She moved just enough to step into his grasp. Slowly, his fingers curled around her arm and more than anything he wanted to pull her in close. His gaze fell to her lips and ached to kiss her.

"Are you sure?" he asked.

"I've never been surer about anything in my life." She leaned in and before he could protest, she kissed him fully on the lips. His hands traveled up her arms and wrapped around her neck, pulling her in tighter as he let his fear go and stepped into the only future he was sure of.

When they separated, they stared into each other's eyes and slowly his lips pulled into a smile. "Have I told you I love you?" he asked.

She pressed her lips into a tight smile. "You might've mentioned it last night, but I plan to hear it over and over again for the rest of my life."

"The rest of your life? That could be a very long time."

She nodded. "And you'll be right beside me."

He could only hope. "But Jodie, what if…?"

"What if we what? What if we spend our days taking care of each other? What if we have beautiful babies? What if we save more lives using the skills that God gave us?

What if we grow old together? If I have only one of these things, then I will consider myself blessed. The question is…will you?"

He reached for her face and traced his thumb over her smooth cheek. "I already am."

She turned her face into his hand and placed a sweet kiss against his fingers. "I bought you a present," she whispered. As she pulled away, he held on to her tight. "I'll be right back. I promise."

She went to the doorway and signed. In the next moment, Shiloh and Cleo came barreling into the room and strapped to their vests were two bouquets of daisies. Jodie plucked one off Shiloh's back and brought it back to him.

Holding it out to him, she said, "I thought we could start over."

Victor felt his face split in a huge smile. He took the flowers from her, remembering the day he had brought her some. "I had so much hope that day. It was a risk, but I was going to take it."

"Take it again, Victor," she whispered.

Breathing deep, he held a single daisy between them. Slowly, he brought it to her ear and tucked it behind it. "This is what I wanted to really do that day." He smiled at her sweet beauty and his heart expanded so much, he thought it would burst. "Jodie," he said on a harsh whisper. He swallowed hard. "I would like to spend the rest of my life with you. Will you marry me and make me the happiest man on earth?"

Jodie beamed brightly. "Yes, I would love to be your wife. And I will love you forever through sickness and in health, and wherever God leads us right to the end."

Victor reached behind her head and pulled her down to his lips for a kiss full of joy and excitement for today and all their days to come.

Just then, a voice cleared in the doorway. Tyson stepped

in as Victor turned to see more and more of the team piling into the room.

"Hope we're not interrupting anything," Tyson said. "We brought Christmas dinner, care of Jodie's mom."

Victor looked for Jodie's mother in the crowd, finding her quickly. She was beautiful, just like her daughter. "It's nice to meet you," he said, not sure what to call her.

She stepped up to his other side of the bed. "Welcome to the family," she signed.

Victor lifted his hand to his lips and signed, "Thank you." And then he knew what he wanted to call her. He lifted his hand to his cheek and signed, "Mother."

Her beaming smile told him all would be well, and judging by the crowd in the room, Victor knew he had found his family and he was finally home.

Jodie hopped up beside him on the bed and settled in with a plate for them to share. She signed for Shiloh and Cleo to join them, and the two dogs hopped up and settled down around their legs.

Victor felt tears prick his eyes and he turned to Jodie. "You did this. You did all this."

She shook her head, dropping her forehead to his. "I was only following God's lead…straight to you. Merry Christmas, love."

"The first of many."

* * * * *

Dear Reader,

I hope you have enjoyed the Rocky Mountain K-9 Unit series this year, as well as Victor and Jodie's story. What a joy it has been to be part of this collection, working closely with all the amazing authors who love to bring you hours of entertainment through their inspiring stories of love and intrigue. I am honored to be a part of the series and honored to bring you this story.

As beautiful as Christmas stories are, I wanted to reflect on the messages of redemption and sacrifice. We all have made split-second decisions that didn't turn out well, but through the power of love and second chances, there can be redemption. I believe Victor earned his, and when it came to making another decision, he willingly made the sacrifice for the good of all. I also believe, Jodie's love was exactly what Victor needed to be championed on to their happily ever after.

I love to hear from readers. Please feel free to send me an email at KatyLee@KatyLeeBooks.com or visit my website at KatyLeeBooks.com.

Peace and joy to you!

Katy Lee

Get 4 FREE REWARDS!

We'll send you 2 FREE Books plus 2 FREE Mystery Gifts.

FREE Value Over **$20**

Both the **Love Inspired®** and **Love Inspired®** Suspense series feature compelling novels filled with inspirational romance, faith, forgiveness, and hope.

HARLEQUIN
PLUS

Announcing a **BRAND-NEW** multimedia subscription service for romance fans like you!

Read, Watch and Play.

Experience the easiest way to get the romance content you crave.

Start your **FREE 7 DAY TRIAL** at
www.harlequinplus.com/freetrial.

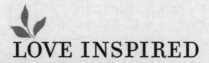

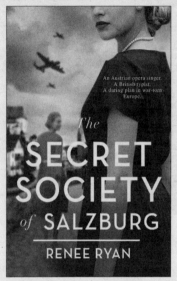